Midnight Prophecy

By

Ellen Dugan

Published by Ellen Dugan

ACKKNOWLEDGMENTS

As always, thanks to my family, friends, beta readers, and editors. To Katie, Michael and Nccole and a special thanks Martha Jane for letting me bounce ideas off of her until I solved the mystery of the Midnight Prophecy.

Other titles by Ellen Dugan

THE LEGACY OF MAGICK SERIES

Legacy Of Magick, Book 1

Secret Of The Rose, Book 2

Message Of The Crow, Book 3

Beneath An Ivy Moon, Book 4

Under The Holly Moon, Book 5

The Hidden Legacy, Book 6

Spells Of The Heart, Book 7

Sugarplums, Spells & Silver Bells, Book 8

Magick & Magnolias, Book 9 (Coming 2018)

Mistletoe & Ivy, Book 10 (Coming 2019)

THE GYPSY CHRONICLES

Gypsy At Heart, Book 1

Gypsy Spirit, Book 2

Book 3 (Coming 2019)

DAUGHTERS OF MIDNIGHT SERIES

Midnight Gardens, Book 1

Midnight Masquerade, Book 2

Midnight Prophecy, Book 3

Take a lover who looks at you like maybe you are magic.

-Frida Kahlo

PROLOGUE

If there's one thing I know, it's magick.

It was an integral part of me, and I'd felt the beat of its rhythm since I was a little girl. Instinctively, I understood its workings, the why and the how. Sitting in the gardens beside my Gran, I was quietly and carefully taught the natural tools of the herbalist's trade. I came to revere the energies of nature, to understand the cycles of the moon and the tides of all four seasons. I learned to respect the elements and the enchantment of tree, flower, and herb.

The roses in the garden could inspire friendship and romance. Lavender was protective and used for cleansing. The oak tree encouraged prosperity and knowledge, while sage brought wisdom and longevity. All of these lessons and many more I soaked up and integrated into my own life. I accepted my place in the overall design of it all and embraced my destiny as a wielder of its power.

Centuries ago they would have called me a Witch, and my fate would not have been kind. Today, the females in my family referred to themselves as wise women, and although the term *wise woman* was often used interchangeably with Witch, they both suited me.

I considered myself a modern practitioner of the Old Ways. With that thought in mind, I decide to honor my family's heritage, combine it with the skills I'd learned in my Gran's kitchen and gardens, and start a business of my own.

It was an irresistible challenge for me...Combining the historic remedies, potions and lotions of the wise woman, and turning it into natural products for the modern consumer. I was thrilled at the opportunity to shake things up and do something different—my pink hair not withstanding.

I was feeling quite proud of myself. My

business proposal had been accepted, and I'd worked hard to save the money required for starting up. With a schedule in place, projected timeline and professional goals all mapped out, *Camilla's Lotions' & Potions* was ready to launch.

As I loaded the last of my stock into the family's old pickup truck, I was excited to begin this new chapter in my life. I certainly wasn't hoping for romance, nor had I ever expected to deal with prophecies and curses. They simply had no room in the personal agenda I had so sensibly organized and cultivated.

However, fate is a tricky beast and sometimes it has other plans for you. Plans you never saw coming, no matter how wise you think you may be.

My name is Camilla Jane Midnight, and this is my story.

CHAPTER ONE

"Cammy, that display looks wonderful!"

I glanced over my shoulder and saw Nicole Dubois. "Thanks, Nicole."

"This is precisely what I had in mind when I talked Max into renting out booth space in the retail area of the garden center." Nicole stopped to stand beside me. "I love how you used the repurposed wooden crates. Very rustic and earthy at the same time."

"That's exactly the vibe I was going for." I smiled at her description and made a few adjustments to the presentation. Two large wooden crates were stacked with the open end out on one side of the sturdy, wooden farmhouse table. The top crate held short rows of my handmade lotions and hand creams. The bottom crate housed bottles of my honey and soapwort shampoo. Next to that were smaller jars of shaving soaps and all-natural body scrubs.

Nicole picked up one of my handmade soaps from the display boxes on the table. She took a long appreciative sniff. "It all smells *fantastic!*"

"Then my master plan is working," I said as she carefully replaced the soap. "I figure the fragrance alone will entice people over to check out the booth."

Nicole ran a hand over her glossy cap of dark hair. "Can I ask where you found these mini wooden boxes?"

The narrow soap boxes she admired allowed for ten bars to be held neatly upright. There were five of them arranged side by side, each holding a different variety. "My grandfather made these for Gran years ago," I explained. "She always used the boxes for her booth at the Farmer's Market." I ran my finger along the edge of the wood. "As I'm the latest member of the family to carry on the daughters of Midnight tradition of selling handmade lotions and soaps, Gran insisted that I incorporate them into my booth for good luck."

Nicole adjusted the white rustic sign at my table. *"Camilla's Lotions & Potions.* The name is both clever and charming."

"That's high praise coming from the PR person." I wiggled my eyebrows, making her chuckle.

"You're going to sell out today," she said. "I have a feeling."

I filled up the clear case that held my lip balms while we chatted. The positive feedback from Nicole was music to my ears. I'd worked my ass off at home, perfecting my products, labels, and overall design of the display. I popped open another cardboard box and lifted out a big metal basket filled with cellophane-wrapped bags of seasonal potpourri. Each bag was tied with a raffia bow and embellished with a bit of seasonal trim.

"What else do you have for us?" Nicole held her hands out to help.

Realizing she was almost as excited as I was, I accepted her enthusiastic assistance. She took the big basket, and I pulled out a divided wooden container that held samples of the potpourri. Working together, we arranged the samples next to the metal basket.

"I made an autumn mix—pumpkin spice and a winter holiday blend." I pointed out how the bags were trimmed differently. "There's waxed oak leaves attached to the autumn's raffia bow and sprigs of silk holly leaves with gold ribbon for the winter variety of potpourri.

"Cammy, that was clever to add seasonal trimming."

"I figured folks would spot the trim on the bows and immediately know which was which." I added tiny clear scoopers to the potpourri sample box.

Nicole took the scooper, lifted some of the autumn mix, and sniffed. "Ooh. I'm going to want some of this for the shop."

"I think that could be arranged," I said, moving the final piece into place. What had started out as an old quilt rack had been upcycled into a bath bomb display stand that now held two rows of small metal pails. I'd affixed labels to the front of each, showing what type of cellophane wrapped bath bomb was inside every bucket.

"If you don't mind me asking, what exactly is a bath bomb?" Nicole said cautiously.

"That's a valid question," I said. "After all, you'll be talking to the customers about them more than I will." I picked up a pink, rose scented one. "Bath bomb 101," I said. "You unwrap one, drop it in the bathwater, wait five minutes, and it makes the water colorful and fizzy. They're fun and relaxing, it softens hard water and they smell great."

"What's in them?" she wanted to know.

"Basically, baking soda, corn starch, Epsom salts, essential oils..." I cut myself off from rattling off the recipe and handed her the wrapped bath item. "All the ingredients are listed on the packaging."

"They're pretty. I like all the different colors," Nicole said, picking up another variety.

I nodded. "They're different fragrances too. We've got orange, lavender, rose, sandalwood, lemon, and last but not least, an oatmeal cocoa butter variety for dry skin."

"Did you remember to bring your business cards?" Nicole asked.

I pulled a stack of them out of my pocket and

handed them over. "Here you go."

"I'll put these at the check-out counter," Nicole took a few steps and stopped. "Don't forget to leave some cards in your booth, as well."

"I'm on it." I smiled and added another stack of cards next to my sign. I stepped back to give the booth a final inspection. I barely resisted bouncing up and down, reminded myself it wasn't professional behavior, and smiled in satisfaction instead. "Alright kids," I said quietly, *"Camilla's Lotions & Potions* is in business."

I gathered all my empty cardboard boxes, stacked them inside of each other, and took them to my truck. I slid the boxes across the passenger seat, shut the door, turned, and bounced off Max Dubois.

"Hi, Cammy." Max reached out to steady me.

"Hey, Max." The owner of the garden center was practically family. He stood there in his jeans and garden center polo, his dark blonde hair curling out slightly from under his ball cap.

"I went ahead and put the hay bale, two cornstalk bundles, purple mums, and the pumpkins you picked out in the truck bed for you," he said.

"Thanks," I said. "I've just finished setting up my booth for tomorrow and was heading up to Gabriella and Philippe's to help them decorate for Halloween."

"Max." Nicole came to the door of the garden center. "Come and see the beautiful display Cammy made for the shop!" she said to her new husband.

Max slung a friendly arm around my shoulders as we walked inside. He stopped in front of the booth and silently looked it over. "This is awesome, Cammy," he said after a moment.

"Thank you for giving me the chance to launch my business."

"You're family." Max smiled. "There's no need to thank us."

"I was going to save this for Saturday..." I said. "But I want to do this now." I reached under the table and pulled out a large gift basket decorated with a burlap bow and silk autumn leaves. Inside the basket nestled in shredded brown craft paper was a large cellophane bag of the autumn mix potpourri, samples of each of the soaps, a bottle of lotion, lip balms, and a few bath bombs too.

"That's so pretty," Nicole said. "I bet folks would like gift baskets for the holiday—"

"This is for you and Max," I said, gently interrupting her.

"What?" Nicole's eyes were round. "Really?"

"It's a thank you gift for allowing me to be your first booth rental client at the garden center." I handed her the decorated basket and watched her smile.

"Cammy," Max protested. "That's too much."

"Nonsense," I said, and reached in the basket for the lip balm I'd made. "Try this, Max, it will help your lips from getting chapped when the weather starts to get cold."

"Thank you, Cammy," Nicole said.

"There's a tinted lip balm in there for you too, Nicole," I said, and smiled when she handed the basket to Max to hold while she began riffling through the contents.

"It has the autumn potpourri and hand cream,

there's gardener's scrubby soap..." Nicole trailed off. "Here it is." She found the tinted lip balm and immediately put some on.

I smiled. "I hope you'll like it."

"It tastes good," she said, running her tongue over her lips.

"It's pomegranate," I explained.

"Let me see." Max leaned over the basket to kiss his bride.

I waited while the newlyweds 'tried' the lip balm. When they came up for air, I smiled. "So, do we both approve?"

"Yes," they said simultaneously, and then laughed.

"I'll see you on Saturday," I told them as we said our goodbyes. I stopped at the door, intending to give Nicole and Max a wave, but they didn't notice. They were too busy smiling into each other's eyes.

People were dropping like flies around here, I thought. *First Dru and Garrett fell for each other. Next Max and Nicole rekindled their romance and married last month, and then Gabriella and Philippe got engaged.* "It's like an epidemic," I said to myself.

I climbed into the truck, started it up, and sang along with the radio as I drove to the Marquette house on Notch Cliff. I turned onto the road, passed a few car-loads of customers from the winery show room that were traveling back the opposite way, and began to smile as the mansion came into view.

"Hello gorgeous," I said with a happy sigh. There were few things I adored more than bedecking a house for Halloween, and my current prospect for seasonal decorating was a life-long architectural crush.

The old stone mansion on Notch Cliff had atmosphere and a *personality,* I'd guess you'd say. I'd been fascinated by the three-story manor for over ten years. Ever since my oldest sister Drusilla had taken me up here on a dare. The mansion had been abandoned at the time, and we'd stumbled up and down stairs with flashlights, poking around. I'd seen my first ghost that night, and I'd been infatuated with the building ever since.

Three stories of local limestone were topped with a tower at the eastern end, and a dramatic roofline. The scaffolds on the west side of the house were still in place from the last of the restoration work, but that only made it spookier —in my opinion. Over the past few months the roof had been repaired, and an ornate wooden porch was starting to be rebuilt. Originally, a covered porch had graced the entire bottom floor of the building. It did my heart good to see the old mansion coming back to life.

I maneuvered slowly past several men who were working on the landscaping crew. They'd been busy adding young trees and shrubs to the grounds in front of the mansion all week. I noted they'd planted oak trees and a few dogwoods. *Those were good choices,* I thought to myself. According to the old traditions, the oak symbolized prosperity, longevity, and strength. While the dogwood represented: love undiminished by adversity.

I lifted my hand in a wave to the crew as I passed. It looked like they were finishing up for the day.

I parked on the gravel drive just past the side entrance that the current occupants used. I hopped out, pocketed the keys in my jeans, and swung around to drop the tailgate. Eyeballing my decorating supplies, I barely resisted rubbing my hands together and letting loose a cackle.

Wise women never cackle, dear. I heard my Gran's voice as surely as if she were standing next to me.

"Okay, okay. No cackling," I said, but couldn't stop the grin.

While situated at the top of the hill, the mansion was in full view of the *Trois Amis* winery gift shop, and it was smart to jazz it up for a couple of reasons. First off, it let customers know that the estate was being lived in again, and secondly, even though there was a sprawling section of lawn between the winery shop and the mansion proper, a lit entrance on the house was good for security purposes.

I glanced over my shoulder, past the landscapers and down the sloping lawn towards the winery showroom. I'd been working there part-time since the opening this past summer, and I'd had a hand in decorating the winery too. Of course, if I'd have had my way, the show room would have gone all out for Halloween. However, the owners and Nicole—the PR person for the winery, had decided to be practical and decorate with a generic autumnal décor that would be suitable for *all* the fall holidays.

Garlands of silk autumn leaves and dangling orange lights were strung across the wine shop entrance. Stacks of pumpkins from Max's garden center were artfully displayed on hay bales, and fat bundles of corn stalks flanked the entrance to the shop. The autumnal display was cheerful and rustic and could stay in place straight through Thanksgiving.

Shifting my attention back to the side entrance of the mansion, I realized that the entire area had been ruthlessly weeded and swept clean. Now you could appreciate the curving brick pathway that led to a landing of more vintage brick, which complimented the wide wooden door.

My sister, Gabriella, had moved in to the restored section of the mansion a couple of weeks ago with her fiancé, Philippe Marquette. Clearly she'd already been at work adding pretty touches to her new home.

Two heavy concrete urns stood empty and

waiting to be filled on either side of the short brick pathway to the private entrance. The wavy old glass windows on either side of the door shone clean in the afternoon light. Sturdy window boxes of reclaimed wood had been added beneath them. Cold-tolerant purple, orange and black pansies filled the boxes and added some brightness against the limestone exterior.

The window boxes had been a gift from our oldest sister Drusilla. Ever the gardener, Dru had planted up the boxes full of the trick-or-treat variety of flowers and installed the rustic boxes herself as a house-warming gift.

I noticed the metal and glass lantern-style fixture flanking the door had recently been revamped too. Once upon a time it would have been hooked up for a gas flame. Now the lantern was wired for electricity, but it still maintained an old-world charm.

Finally, a new small planting bed had been tucked in along one side of the brick landing and pathway. A handsome Japanese Maple tree had been added, a half-dozen purple chrysanthemums were planted in the garden to keep the tree company, and the plot was freshly mulched.

"Hi!" A happy, young voice sounded to my left.

I spun from my inspection of the side entrance and discovered a blonde haired little boy. "Hello, there," I said.

"Are you the lady?" he asked. "I brought you some more toys."

I estimated him to be around five years old. He wore a bright t-shirt, denim jacket, and his jeans were caked with mud at the knees. I wondered where his parents were. I hunkered down to his level. "I'm Camilla. Who are you?"

"I'm Jaime." His bright laughter bubbled up. "You have pink hair."

I pulled a section of it in front of my face and squinted one eye in concentration. "Well..." I said, as if amazed. "What do you know?"

"Why is it pink?" he wanted to know.

"Because I like it." I winked at him.

"You're funny," the child said.

"Where's your mom and dad, Jaime?" I asked automatically.

"My daddy is over there." He pointed down

the hill.

I stood and checked in the direction he'd pointed, and sure enough a man was hustling up the slope. "Jaime Alexander!" he called.

The boy waved. "Over here, daddy!"

The man walked closer, and my eyes widened with appreciation. He was tall, built, and wearing the khaki uniform shirt of the landscaping team. His old jeans were white at the stress points, and he wore sturdy boots. His hair was the same dark blonde as his son's, but was cut short and neat with enough to tumble over his forehead. "Wow," I said under my breath, admiring the man's long-legged stride.

"I told you not to wander off," the man said to the boy.

"I came to see if Miss Ella had any more cookies." Jaime leaned against me and smiled innocently at his father.

With an exasperated breath, the man pulled off his sunglasses. "I'm sorry," he said. "He knows not to come up here alone."

The father's eyes were a warm blue, and when our eyes met I felt a hitch under my heart. Jaime's daddy was sexy as hell. *Please be single!* I thought, and tried a smile. "Hello." I rested my hand on the boy's head. "I'm Camilla Midnight."

Jaime tipped his face to mine. "Camilla." He pronounced it carefully.

I winked down at him. "My friends call me Cammy."

"Miss Ella says her name is Gabriella." Jaime hooked a thumb at his chest. "But *I* get to call her Ella."

"I'm Jacob," the man said, introducing himself. "I know you," he said, and tugged off a work glove before offering his hand. The casual gesture had my stomach flipping. "You're Drusilla and Gabriella's sister. I work with Max at the garden center."

Jacob gave my hand the briefest of squeezes. It was perfectly socially acceptable, yet I felt it all the way to my toes. There was something about him...something intriguing. Belatedly, I remembered to let go of his hand. With an effort I dragged my eyes from his face and tried to pull my thoughts back in line. "You work at the garden center?"

"That's right." One corner of his mouth

kicked up. "I run the landscaping crew for Max," he said.

By the goddess, I thought. *How had I missed seeing him over the past few weeks?*

Behind us, the door opened with a dramatic creak and my sister popped her head out. "Hey, Cammy," Gabriella said.

"Hi, Ella. You have visitors."

Gabriella stepped out carrying a box of lights and Halloween accessories. She spotted Jaime and Jacob and smiled. "Hi guys!"

Jaime zipped over to Gabriella's side. "Whatcha doing?"

"Cammy is going to help me decorate for Halloween," she told him.

"I'm going to be the Flash for Halloween!" Jaime announced.

I took the box of decorations from my sister. "That sounds pretty cool," I said to the boy.

Gabriella pulled a plastic sandwich bag out of her jacket pocket. "As promised," she said, handing Jaime a bag of sugar cookies.

"Thanks!" Jaime hugged Gabriella. "I like the orange sprinkles!"

"I'll take those," Jacob said, and nipped the

cookies from his son.

"Awww, *Dad*!" Jaime complained.

"You can have them tonight, *after* your dinner." Jacob took his son's hand. "Say good night to Miss Ella and Miss Cammy."

Jaime grinned and waved. "Bye!"

"Nice to meet you." I smiled, and did my best not to sigh over them as father and son walked back down the hill. "Those two are seriously adorable." I whispered to my sister.

"Jaime's a cutie," Gabriella agreed.

"So is his daddy." I sighed anyway, enjoying the view of Jacob's backside as he walked away.

Gabriella smiled at me. "I seem to recall you giving me this speech about focusing on your business and avoiding romance for the foreseeable future."

"I *am* focusing on my business, but when a guy like that strolls into your day, you should take a moment and appreciate." I waited a beat. "Do you know if he's single?"

Gabriella smiled. "I'm pretty sure he is."

I shifted the box of decorations under one arm. "No baby mama in the picture?"

"Not that I've heard," Gabriella said.

"Who'd walk away from *that*?" I asked.

"I know, right?" Gabriella agreed. "Regardless, Jacob is a great father."

I slanted my eyes over at my sister. "You have details. Gimme."

"Jacob and his son live in the village at his parent's house," Gabriella said. "Jaime is five and goes to morning Kindergarten. Jacob has had his son with him the last few afternoons because his parents are out of town."

I grinned. "I knew you'd have the scoop."

"I *know* because I offered to let Jaime hang out with me the other day when it was raining," Gabriella explained. "We baked cookies. Then Philippe showed him around the ballroom. Philippe was adorable with him."

I patted my sister's baby bump. "Practicing, were you?"

She laughed. "Being around Jaime the past few days, has sort of given me a preview of what to expect when my little guy is older."

"Girl," I said. "I keep telling you, it's a girl."

"There hasn't been a female born in the Marquette line in generations," Gabriella reminded me. "Odds are, it's a boy."

CHAPTER TWO

My eyes traveled down the hill. I watched Jacob scoop his son up and haul him to his work truck. Jaime's laughter traveled up to me. Smiling over the happy sound, I turned back to Gabriella. "Anyway, your side entrance to the mansion is looking great."

"I've been working on it, with a lot of help from Jacob and the landscaping crew."

I nodded toward the Japanese Maple. "Baby's hands," I said, referring to the tree's meaning in the language of flowers. "That's cute, *and* a good choice for this side of the house. The tree will stay small and the purple-red leaves are gorgeous."

Gabriella pointed at the mulched bed. "Philippe helped me plant crocus, early daffodils and red tulip bulbs around the edge the other day. By time the baby is born the crocus and daffodils will be blooming all along the brick path."

"Hope, chivalry, and an ardent love...that's quite the magickal combination you've added with those flowers to your garden, Sis."

Gabriella chuckled. "I honestly wasn't thinking about the language of flowers at the time...more like what would be pretty when the baby arrived." She waited a beat. "But a touch of wise woman's magick certainly wouldn't hurt this place."

"The purple mums give the bed some nice fall color." I said.

"And they also add 'cheer'," Gabriella acknowledged.

"The garden may be small, but it's enchanting, Ella."

Gabriella smiled at the compliment. "The side entrance is looking so much better that I decided to go ahead and decorate. I'm not sure if we'll get trick-or-treaters up here...but, I thought it would be fun."

"I'll bet you get some kids. I don't think they

could resist coming up here on Halloween." I said. "Especially now that it feels more like an entrance to a real home instead of a..."

"Horror movie?" Gabriella said, pulling on a pair of thin gardening gloves.

"I *love* this place," I said, setting the box on the ground. "It's so gothic and full of history. How goes living in spook central?"

"Interesting," Gabriella said. "There are lots of noises to get used to in there."

"Have you seen anything yet?"

"Maybe. I'm not sure." Gabriella shrugged. "I thought I heard someone walking in the western wing the other night. Also, there's a few places in the mansion that make me feel incredibly sad.

"Sounds like a classic residual style haunt." I said.

Gabriella nodded. "It takes some getting used to knowing you're not alone in the house."

"Are your impressions that the ghost is male or female?"

"That's something we'd like your opinion on," she said. "I figured since you've worked with that paranormal team, that you'd be the person to ask." Gabriella shrugged. "Maybe you can figure out who the ghost is and why they are still around."

"I'd love that," I said, tipping my head back and studying the stone structure. "This old house has such an interesting vibe."

"There's a lot to discover in the house and the grounds. Like those planters," Gabriella said. "They were out back, completely covered in ivy. I cut the vines back, scrubbed them up, and had Philippe bring them around to the entrance for me."

"They make a dramatic statement." I pulled a bag of potting soil out of the truck and hauled it over to one of the urns. "Plus, if you tried to buy them new, they'd cost a fortune."

Gabriella followed me back to the truck. "Philippe's starting to get tired of me digging through the property and asking him to haul more of my finds over to our side of the house."

"Treasure hunting, eh?"

"You bet." Gabriella grinned. "I found a set of blue willow dishes in the house too. I washed them by hand and added them to the hutch in the kitchen. Oh, and the other day I uncovered this winged gargoyle out back. He's going to look great out front for Halloween."

"I can't wait to see it." I grabbed a second large bag of potting mix.

Gabriella reached in the back of the truck and pulled out two containers of purple mums. "The winged statue was covered in weeds and honeysuckle vine. I bet he was guarding a pond at one time. But that's all been filled in now."

"Maybe I can find some old drawings or photos of the grounds when I start researching," I said, and proceeded to fill up the urns with potting mix.

"It would be interesting to see how the grounds were laid out long ago," Gabriella agreed.

After filling up the urns with potting soil, I tugged the hay bale out of the truck. With a grunt I swung it down and placed it on the left side of the brick landing. I brushed loose straw from my black t-shirt. While Gabriella tucked her new mums in the large urns, I added a few bundles of cornstalks to flank the doorway. Chatting with my sister, I secured the cornstalks in place with floral wire.

"Here comes Philippe." Gabriella flashed a grin over her shoulder. "He's bringing the gargoyle around now in the wheelbarrow. And he's muttering—in French. He must be pretty annoyed with me."

"Oh please." I rolled my eyes as the sound of gravel crunching underfoot carried closer. "The man would do anything you asked him."

Gabriella patted her baby bump. "All I have to do is act like I'm about to lift something."

"That's devious, Ella." I wiped an imaginary tear from my eye. "I'm so proud."

"Gabriella," Philippe huffed, straining to keep the wheelbarrow from tipping. "I have the *gargouille*."

"Gar-gooey," Gabriella said, pronouncing the word carefully. "I can actually remember that one."

I smiled at the exchange between them. Philippe was determined that Gabriella should learn French, and my sister was refusing to take formal classes. While they lightheartedly argued over her stubbornness I helped Philippe lift the stone gargoyle, and we maneuvered it into place to the right side of the door.

"Maybe you can call the gargoyle, Louie?" I suggested after we had the statue in the spot my sister preferred. "You know, because it rhymes. Louie the gar-gooey."

Gabriella burst out laughing. "Didn't you have an ancestor with that name?" she asked Philippe.

Philippe smiled. "I did. Louis would be a good middle name for our son."

I crossed my arms. "I still say it's a girl."

Gabriella tucked a couple of gourds into the pot with the mums. "We'll find out *if* Philippe is right on Friday at the ultrasound appointment."

"*Ma belle*," Philippe raised an eyebrow at my sister. "You need to get used to saying: Yes Philippe, you are right."

With a laugh, Philippe caught the mini pumpkin that Gabriella threw at him.

"I'll bet you five bucks," I said, unwrapping the orange outdoor lights, "that the baby *is* a girl."

"I will take that bet." Philippe smiled.

"And if it's a girl, you have to name her after me." I gave the Frenchman a playful jab with my elbow.

Gabriella rolled her eyes at the two of us as we joked about the gender of the baby. With her direction, we added a garland of fall foliage and a strand of orange lights around the doorway. She took another strand of orange lights and looped it over and around the pumpkins on the hay bale. As a finishing touch, Gabriella tucked a silly wooden Halloween sign in the bale. It was tall, glittery and bright in purple, green, and orange, and pointed the way to a few different roads: *Boo Boulevard, Witch Way*, and *Trick or Treat Street*.

By the time Philippe plugged the lights to a big outdoor extension cord and a timer, it was dusk. Gabriella made a few adjustments to the lights, and I tucked the extension cord behind the hay bale for her.

"So," I asked as we finished up, "how do you suppose the ghost will react to the Halloween decorations?"

Philippe tucked an arm around Gabriella's waist. "I imagine we will soon find that out as well."

"Tell me all about it," I said. "Over supper."

I'd been in the mansion a few times before—not counting my ghostly adventure when I was fourteen. This past summer Philippe had given the winery employees an abbreviated tour of the house. He'd shown us all the areas he was converting into an event venue—with the idea that when the winery customers asked about the restorations we would be able to tell them the plans for the property. I'd been back again a few weeks ago, on the day we helped Gabriella move in.

In the future, they would hold events on the opposite side of the mansion from where Gabriella and Philippe lived. The old ballroom on the first floor of the western wing and several other rooms were currently being restored for both ceremony and wedding reception areas. In addition, the formal western terraces where the Masquerade Party had been held were also being spruced up for future outdoor weddings, and other occasions.

The plans for the mansion were ambitious, but it was a way to make the estate pay for itself. I didn't even want to know how much Philippe had invested into the winery, and now the restoration of his ancestral home.

Philippe and Gabriella had claimed several renovated rooms as their personal living space on the second and third floors of the eastern wing. Their side entrance opened onto a lobby, and this part of the eastern wing hosted a formal client area. Philippe's office was on the first floor, along with an office for Nicole—the winery's PR person. In addition, there was a small meeting room and a restroom.

You had to travel up the massive wooden staircase to gain access to the private area that now belonged to Gabriella and Philippe. On the second-floor landing, a big panel of plywood had been secured over the missing section of a stained-glass window. It would be breathtaking when it was restored. But for now, the plywood kept it all from being too intimidating, in my opinion.

On the second floor there was a spacious, brand new kitchen that opened onto a cozy living room and a powder room. Three large bedrooms and two full baths were situated on the third floor, and finally, at the farthest, eastern point of the third floor, was the tower.

The round room was both dramatic and gothic. Philippe used the space as a sort of library and den.

It was absolutely my favorite of all the renovated rooms. The walls were paneled in rich, dark wood. The fireplace was huge and made from local stone. Displayed above the mantle was a recently restored portrait of one of Philippe's ancestors, Pierre Michel Marquette. Pierre had been younger than I was now when he'd had his portrait painted. He'd been portrayed as handsome, standing in front of his family's home. Yet there was something about his expression that told me he'd been trouble.

Over dinner, Philippe filled me in on his family history with regards to the house, and the two brothers—Claude and Pierre Michel— who had lived there in the 1840's. It was Claude, the eldest of the brothers, who'd been Philippe's great, great, great grandfather.

"Claude and his wife lived here with their boys, as well," Gabriella said, serving her herbed chicken stew. "Three of their five sons were born here."

"They had *five* boys?" I asked.

"I told you." Gabriella sat, and rested her hands over her baby bump. "There's been no females born into his family line in several generations."

Philippe smiled at her and continued the tale. "According to the Marquette family history, Pierre Michel—"

"The smug guy in the portrait," I clarified.

"Yes." Philippe nodded. "He had been strong-armed into an arranged marriage with a local girl from a wealthy family. Pierre Michel and his bride lived in the mansion for a while...actually, a very brief period," Philippe explained. "For not long after the wedding, Bridgette Ames and her dowry disappeared."

"Wait," I stopped Philippe. "Ames, as in Ames Crossing?"

He nodded. "That is correct."

"The Ames family owned everything, back in the day," I said. "Bridgette's disappearance must have been a scandal of major proportions."

Philippe passed me a dinner roll. "Pierre Michel was suspected of doing away with his wife, yet he was never arrested."

"Well yeah. No body equals no murder," I said, buttering the roll. "It's not like they had C.S.I. back then."

"The story goes that the Ames family put a lot of pressure on the Marquettes." Philippe sampled his chicken stew. "However, the story had a tragic ending for both of the families. Six months after Bridgette disappeared, Pierre Michel was killed in an accident."

"No wonder the house is haunted," I said to Philippe. "Classically, hauntings are caused by a violent death, or a traumatic event."

"Thanks, Cammy." Gabriella shuddered. "That is *not* going to help me sleep tonight."

"Maybe the woman in white I saw all those years ago was Bridgette Ames." I drummed my fingers on the kitchen table as I thought it over.

Philippe leaned forward. "Gabriella mentioned you had an experience when you were younger."

"I was fourteen, and fearless—at least I was until I saw her. When she spoke to me, I screamed and went running back to Drusilla as fast as I could." I smiled at the memory. "Seeing that manifestation is what got me interested in paranormal investigations." I admitted.

Philippe narrowed his eyes in concentration. "What did she say?"

"She said..." I paused for dramatic effect. "*The prophecy awaits.*"

"That is beyond creepy." Gabriella hunched her shoulders. "What did she look like exactly?"

I smiled at my sister. "She had long dark hair and was wearing a white gown, with puffy sleeves."

"Where were you in the house when you saw her?" Philippe asked.

"I was in the western side of the building, on the third floor."

"Sections of the staircase between the second and third floors have been missing for years. They weren't even replaced until recently." Philippe frowned at me. "You could have been injured, Camilla."

I propped my chin in my hand and fluttered my lashes at him. "Your accent gets thicker when you are annoyed."

Philippe gave me a serious look. "Camilla,"

he began.

"Oh wow." I pressed my hand to my heart. "I've never heard my name pronounced that way. Cam-ee-ya," I sounded it out.

"*Parfait.*" Philippe dropped his head in his hands. "Now I have *deux femme têtues* to deal with."

"Wait, wait," I said. "I took a couple of years of French in school. I think I can figure that out. "*Parfait*—perfect. *Deux femme*— Two women...you said, two 'stubborn' women?"

Philippe began to laugh. "*Combien de français connaissez-vous?*"

"How much French do I know?" I repeated back to him.

"Oh dear goddess," Gabriella said, shaking her head. "I'm never going to hear the end of this."

"*Je connais un peu de français*" I said to Philippe, holding my thumb and first finger close together.

"What does that mean?" Gabriella asked me.

I raised one eyebrow at my sister. "It means: I know a little French."

***

After dinner Gabriella and I sat together on their big leather sofa in the tower room. Shadow the cat had made the move with Gabriella, and he was currently sprawled across the top of an upholstered wing backed chair. His fluffy self seemed to defy gravity as he balanced across the back of the chair.

Philippe had volunteered to do kitchen clean up, and he'd promised to bring in some of his own research to share with me. I propped my feet on the coffee table and studied the portrait of Philippe's three times great uncle and wondered what the old boy thought of being part of the Halloween decorations.

Gabriella had set up a stylish Halloween vignette in silver, black and white across the heavy mantle and beneath the old portrait. Creamy white pumpkins in an assortment of shapes and sizes were nestled in a bed of sphagnum moss. A cracked, black painted urn had been pressed into duty. It was missing a handle, yet it stood tall on one end of the mantle. Spilling out of the opening of the urn was more moss with a plump white Cinderella pumpkin nesting on top. A faded black silk top hat rested over the stem of the pumpkin.

Candle holders of all different shapes and sizes held LED candles. Antique tarnished silver frames displayed small black and white vintage clip art of cats, witches, and bats. A few artificial crows perched in the moss, and another on top of a stack of timeworn books. Gabriella hadn't been kidding when she said she'd been treasure hunting in the old house. She'd used her finds and put them to excellent use creating an elegantly spooky seasonal display.

At the moment my sister held a notebook in her lap. It was filled with paint swatches and photos of gray area rugs, a few different styles of white cribs, and snowy dressers. Gabriella was starting to plot out her baby's nursery.

"What do you think of these wall colors?" she asked.

I raised my eyebrow at the soft tones ranging from sky blue to pale aqua. "Ella, those paint samples are all blue."

She narrowed her eyes at me. "Yes, I know. I

like them, and the painter is coming the day after tomorrow. I'd do it, but Philippe worries about me being around the fumes."

I patted her arm. "It won't hurt to let someone else paint the walls."

"I'd rather take care of it myself," she argued.

"Um hmm," I made a sound of agreement, taking the paint samples. "Let's see."

I restrained myself from telling my sister she was going to have to repaint when she found out the baby was a girl...and instead, considered something else. I'd had a few dreams about seeing Gabriella sitting in a tufted chair, holding her daughter in a faery-tale themed nursery. I hadn't shared *that* information with my sister. However...

One of the shades of blue reminded me of the dress she'd worn to the masquerade party this summer. Gabriella had looked a bit like a modern-day Cinderella in the gown, and it was the night she and Philippe had met and fallen for each other. What could make a more perfect faery-tale nursery theme for their little girl?

I pointed out the color on her paint swatches

that reminded me most of the blue of her dress. "That one." I said. "It's somewhere between pastel aqua and dusty blue. It would go great with pale gray and white."

Gabriella drew a star on the swatch. "That one is my favorite as well." Satisfied, she tucked away her notebook and swatches.

I made a mental note to search for some vintage Cinderella-themed wall art. I had also recently seen a way to make a pretty, silver and sparkly pumpkin out of the foam pumpkins they sold at the arts and craft store for Halloween. That would be a fun project to make for the baby's room. My future niece deserved a bit of faery tale magick in her nursery, and I was just the aunt to give it to her.

I smiled at my sister as she talked about adding a nautical touch to her son's room. *Not this time, Gabriella.* I knew it as surely as I knew my middle name was Jane. Their next child was destined to be a boy...But the baby on the way, the first one, she was definitely a girl.

It would be fun to see their reactions when they found that out for themselves.

CHAPTER THREE

Philippe walked into the tower room with a folder. "I made copies of my research. Both on the history of the house and its former occupants. These are for you," he said, handing them over.

"Excellent." I accepted them happily.

"I thought perhaps with your degree in History you might be able to find out more information than I had been able to gather."

"I can check the local genealogical library, and the Alton and Jersey county historical society," I said, flipping through the papers. There was an architectural drawing with the proposed renovation plans for the mansion and a copy of an old black and white photo of the house dated 1901, culled from the town's historical society. The photo, Philippe explained, was allowing them to accurately re-create the details of the big covered porch on the first floor. There was also a drawing of the original layout of the mansion, and an oversized family tree of the Marquettes.

My lips twitched as I scanned the last several generations of Marquettes. As Philippe had said, there wasn't a single female born into the family line since the early 1800's. I found Claude and Pierre Michel Marquette on the family tree. Claude's wife was named Amelia and their sons were listed. I read the boys' names with amusement: Claude Jr., Tomas, Henri, Lucan, and Archer.

"So what about Claude, Amelia and their family? How did they fare after the big scandal in 1847?" I asked Philippe.

"According to my grandfather, Claude and his family closed up the house and moved back to France."

"Is that oral family history, or do you have actual documentation of when they left the area?" I asked.

"It is a story handed down, but Claude and

Amelia's fourth and fifth sons were both born in France." Philippe said.

Silently, I studied the portrait above the fireplace and wondered what I would find when I started researching the history of the mansion.

Philippe stood with his back to the fireplace. With him standing under the painting, I could see a bit of resemblance to his ancestor in the old portrait...but in the shape of the eyes, and the dark coloring only. Philippe was brawny, while Pierre Michel Marquette had been portrayed as very slim. There had been a definite self-importance and a real conceit portrayed in the subject's expression. His modern-day descendant, on the other hand, was a good man. Philippe was kind and loving. I had no worries about my sister's happiness or their future together as a family.

"Claude never returned to Illinois," Philippe continued to tell me about his family. "However, his third son Henri came back during the 1870's. It was Henri who planted the vineyards and he and his son, Louis, ran them successfully until the 1920's."

"That's when prohibition hit," I realized.

"That was a death knell for the wineries."

"Yes," Philippe agreed. "The vineyards were neglected, and the house fell into disrepair. Out of money and options, my great-great grandfather was quite elderly when he abandoned the property and moved back to France."

I re-checked the family tree, intending to study Philippe's branch in particular, when Shadow decided to abandon his perch and join me on the sofa. The cat hopped up in my lap and sat on my thigh as if studying the oversized page with me.

"Make yourself at home, Shadow." I dropped a kiss on the tabby's head. The cat chirped and swatted at the page. "Be nice." I began to pull the paper farther out of his reach and he pawed at the same section of the page, again. I focused on that area and my eyes zeroed in on something very intriguing. The date for Pierre Michel's death was listed as: October 31, 1847.

My eyes shifted from the date to the cat's face.

"*Meow*." Shadow sounded very smug.

I nodded to the cat in acknowledgement.

"Gabriella." I pitched my voice low. "According to this, Pierre Michel Marquette died on the thirty-first of October."

"He did?" Gabriella leaned forward to see for herself. "By the moon and stars," she breathed. "He died on Samhain?"

Slowly my eyes traveled to the portrait above the fireplace. Pierre stood, painted with the mansion at his back, smirking down at me. I wondered if he was still so arrogant when he was accused of murdering his bride.

"Is that date significant?" Philippe asked.

I slid my eyes back to my sister's. Her expression was guarded. *This wasn't the time or the place to get into metaphysics,* I decided. I cleared my throat. "Interesting, more like." Carefully, I folded the large paper in thirds, and slipped the family tree back in the folder.

"Is something wrong?" Philippe asked.

I flashed him a bright smile. "How about you give me a tour of the western wing before I head home?"

We had to go down to the first floor to access the western two-thirds of the house. Shadow pranced along, as if he were a feline tour guide.

Philippe explained to me that he'd purposefully had the contractors wall off his section of the mansion to keep it private.

While Philippe explained about fire walls and extra insulation, I followed the couple down the hall. The electricity was running on the first floor, and these rooms were in various states of repair. Philippe said that the plaster was being mended and I was happy they were working to restore the home—instead of simply doing a modern renovation.

He showed me a few areas where the woodwork was being repaired wherever possible and being rebuilt where it wasn't. He was working with local craftsmen, and they were taking the time to duplicate the woodwork and experimenting with stains to match the original color.

The ballroom walls were smooth and freshly repainted. On the opposite wall from where we were standing, large picture windows opened up the space. The hardwood floors were being worked on, and they'd been sanded back to the bare wood. I saw several extra boards leaning out against the wall with a variety of stains, and

Philippe explained they were going to choose the most period-accurate color out of the bunch.

"This will be a gorgeous room for wedding receptions," I said.

"That's the plan." Gabriella nodded. "If we could book a dozen weddings next year it would go a long way towards paying for most of the restoration expenses."

"I'll bet Nicole can work her PR mojo and get you several events." I sent Philippe an arch look. "What about your own wedding in June? Will you do that here?"

"I'd want an outdoor ceremony if possible," Gabriella said immediately.

"*Ma belle*," Philippe ran his hand down my sister's arm. "We certainly can, however..." Gabriella sighed loudly over his words, even as he continued. "We should use the occasion of our wedding to—"

"Show off the property," she finished for him.

"*Exactement*," Philippe said.

"Exactly—I agree." I nodded. "It's a smart way to get the locals talking about the mansion as an event venue."

Gabriella hunched her shoulders. "You sounded like Nicole when you said that."

"It is shrewd." I pointed out to her. "If you held the reception indoors, *after* your outdoor ceremony, then you could accomplish both. A two-for-one kind of deal."

"Whose side are you on?" Gabriella asked me.

"You're so damn cute and grumpy when you're pregnant." I smiled at my sister. "I think I'm going to make you some chamomile-based potpourri. You can set it around your rooms, and the scent will make things more peaceful and calm. Maybe it will help you find your inner Zen."

"I'd like some of that," Philippe chuckled. "How soon can you make some for us?"

"You two are a laugh-riot." Gabriella scowled at us both. "First we have the baby," she said. "Then we can hash out all the details for the wedding."

I raised an eyebrow. "I'd get those wedding details nailed down while you can, Gabriella."

"We will," Philippe assured me, and passed out flashlights for everyone.

"I have a baby's room to get ready," Gabriella reminded us. "That comes first."

"Of course it does," I said soothingly. "You're a hearth and home practitioner. For you, having your home in order comes before anything else."

Gabriella tossed her wavy blonde hair over her shoulder. "At least *somebody* gets that."

Gabriella stomped up the stairs, and Shadow bounded up beside his mistress. I slanted my eyes over to Philippe. "She can be very stubborn," I warned him.

He rolled his eyes to the ceiling. "We have been going round and round about this," he said.

"Let her get the baby's room ready first," I suggested. "Then she'll be more inclined to tackle all the details of the wedding."

"Are you two coming or what?" Gabriella called down the stairs.

Together Philippe and I started up the stairs. The staircase on the western side of the mansion was the twin of the stairs in the eastern wing. The risers, as Philippe had said, had been recently repaired. The missing sections of the banisters had been duplicated too and were awaiting fresh stain. I saw that several new floorboards had been feathered into the second-floor landing, where Gabriella stood waiting for us.

"The last time I was this far up into the house, it had been all holes and gaps in the steps and landing," I told them, admiring the restoration.

Gabriella pointed the beam of her flashlight at the glass. "Look, Cammy."

Here the stain glass panels were intact. They featured a central *fleur de lis* in a cloudy blue—similar to the logo for the winery. Four rosettes, one at each corner of the panel, completed the design. It was a simple scheme, but the old glass was fabulous, making the impact of the window much more effective.

I calculated the position of the window. "I bet this lights up every night and is gorgeous at sunset."

"We are having the broken stained-glass panel in our section of the house rebuilt," Philippe explained. "The glass artist is using this window as a template to try and match the designs." He took Gabriella's arm as we traveled farther up to the third floor.

Here, the steps were all brand spanking new, I noted. The wood was still unstained. To protect the raw wood, we stayed on the heavy brown paper that had been attached with blue painter's tape to the center of the treads.

"I took a few photos of the stained-glass myself and added it to the information page on the website about the restoration of the mansion," Gabriella said.

"I certainly hope your boss gave you a raise for that idea." I glanced meaningfully at Philippe.

"True genius is never appreciated in its own time," Gabriella said, straight-faced.

Philippe smiled. "It was Gabriella's idea that we have the stained-glass window professionally photographed to use in advertising for our future event and wedding brochures."

"Smart." I nodded to my sister. "That's a unique and historic touch for your venue. I have a feeling prospective brides will go crazy wanting to be photographed with the pretty vintage stained-glass window illuminated behind them."

When we gained the third floor, Gabriella pulled a dust mask out of her back pocket. She held the mask over her mouth and nose, and as I studied the third floor, I could see why.

The damage to this section of the house had been extensive.

"Now that the roof is whole, the renovations to the third floor will begin early next year," Philippe said. "We had to deal with mold abatement this summer, and then running industrial de-humidifiers, as well."

It made me sad to see that all that remained of the original papered walls was a stained, shredded mess.

I walked down the main hallway, and the cat came along with me. I shined my flashlight into a few rooms and saw a couple of stone fireplaces, one had a tile surround and its mantle was still intact, the rest were pretty rough. It was all empty, though. Still and quiet.

As in no vibrations, and no stray energy hanging around. I hadn't expected the ghost I'd seen over a decade before to pop up simply because I was back on the third floor. Yet, I squelched down a bit of disappointment. *Had the construction made the ghosts shy?* I wondered. Typically, restoration made ghosts more active, as they didn't care for the disruption on their turf.

"Bridgette?" I whispered the name. "Are you here?"

I held my breath, but the only sounds I heard were Philippe and Gabriella talking at the top of the stairs. I told myself not to be impatient and walked back to where my sister and her fiancé waited. One of my pink sneakers caught a buckled floor board. I tripped, caught myself against the wall, and sent the cat scrambling away from me and back down the staircase.

"Are you okay?" Gabriella asked.

"I'm fine," I assured her, and shined the flashlight down. "Will you be able to save the hardwood floors?" I asked.

"We're going to try." Gabriella's voice was muffled from under the mask.

"Is it safe for me to be up here?" I asked Philippe as we started back down to the main floor.

"It is now." Philippe helped Gabriella down the stairs. My lips twitched when she didn't yank away from him, Gabriella wasn't big on people hovering. I smiled fully when Philippe took me by the elbow as well. It was adorable the way the Frenchman was acting all protective of me and my sister.

"All I ask is that you let me know when you'll be here," Philippe said, once we were back on the first floor. "I'll want to make sure you won't be disturbed."

"That's code for: 'that way he can keep an eye on you'." Gabriella used air quotes.

I patted Philippe's arm. "*Ne t'inquiète pas mon beau-frère.*"

In response, he slung an arm around my shoulders and gave me a one-armed hug.

"What the hell does that mean?" Gabriella started to laugh.

I flashed a grin. "I told him: 'don't worry my brother-in-law'."

***

A few days after my visit to the mansion I

was home conjuring up some pretty melt-and-pour soaps to add to my booth. I liked to use molds for variety, and the moon and sun celestial design had been popular this summer when I'd first tried my wares out at the Farmer's Market.

It was my turn to cook supper, and I planned to make turkey meatloaf and mashed potatoes. I put the meatloaf together, peeled the potatoes and put them on to boil. Letting myself out the back door, I picked the last of the fall crop of green beans that Gran had planted. I had enough for several people by the time I was finished, and with a sudden intuitive hunch I knew we were going to need more potatoes too.

I started the beans, peeled more potatoes, and had everything simmering nicely. I moved the trays holding my soap molds to the table in the laundry room to allow them to finish setting up and made a note to order more of the goat's milk soap base. Checking my watch, I pulled out frozen dinner rolls and put them on a baking sheet.

"Supper in fifteen!" I called out, sliding the rolls in with the meatloaf.

"It smells good in here," Dru said, and she began setting the table.

"Has anyone heard from Gabriella today?" Gran asked, coming in from the living room.

"Nope," I said. "Not yet, but I have a feeling." I swung my eyes over to her first ultrasound picture that I'd taped to the fridge back in August. "Dru, you're going to want to get out two more place settings."

"I know her appointment was this afternoon." Drusilla went to the cabinet and pulled down more plates. "I hope everything is okay."

"I'm sure it's fine," Gran said to Dru. "Don't worry."

I drained the potatoes, added butter and grated parmesan cheese. I had only begun mashing them when the kitchen door swung open.

Gabriella poked her head in. "Hi!" she said.

Philippe walked in behind her. "*Bonjour.*"

Gabriella sniffed the air. "By the goddess. Is that meatloaf?"

I smiled. "It is, and parmesan mashed potatoes. Do you want to stay for supper?"

"You bet I do," Gabriella patted her belly. "We're starved."

"How did the ultrasound appointment go?" Dru asked her.

Gabriella took a seat at the table and folded her arms over her baby bump. "Philippe has something to tell everyone," she said.

I stopped to face them. Silently, Philippe tugged his wallet out of his back pocket. With a straight face he pulled out a five dollar bill and handed it to me.

"I *knew* it!" I laughed and threw my arms around his neck.

"What?" Drusilla demanded. "Oh my god." Dru pressed her hand to her mouth. "Are you having twins?"

"No!" Gabriella snorted with laughter. "Just one, and I have the photos to prove it." She pulled ultrasound photos out of her purse.

"It seems," Philippe said, grinning at Gabriella, "that this one time, I was wrong. We are having a *girl*!"

The insanity that followed their announcement was loud and filled with kisses, laughter, and hugs.

While Gran and Drusilla cried happy tears, I went upstairs to my room and pulled out the big gift bag I had stashed in my closet the day before. I walked back in the room and handed the bag to my sister. "Here you go, Mum. Now that you've had what I've been telling you confirmed, you can add this to the nursery."

"Oh no!" Gabriella began to laugh. "The nursery was painted blue. A baby girl's room can't be blue, can it?"

"Maybe," I said. "I had a dream about you sitting in your new nursery a couple of weeks ago, and the room was all soft and pretty, like a faery tale. Anyway, it got me to thinking."

She pushed the tissue paper aside and pulled out the sign I'd had a local craftsperson make. The wooden sign was Cinderella-inspired. It had a sort of shabby chic style, was crackle painted in a pastel blue, and there was a white castle in the background. Stenciled in gothic lettering, it read: 'A Dream Is A Wish Your Heart Makes'.

"Oh, Cammy." Gabriella started to sniffle.

"There's more," I said.

Gabriella handed the sign to Philippe and

dug deeper into the bag. She pulled out a large, sparkling, white foam pumpkin that I'd bedazzled with silver glitter and iridescent beads. Gabriella scanned the gift tag attached to the stem. "For your little pumpkin," she read out loud.

Gran smiled. "That's why I found glitter all over my kitchen floor the other day."

"Damn it, Camilla Jane," Gabriella said, as tears started to roll. "You're making me cry."

"Do you like it?" I asked her.

"Are you kidding?" she said, wiping her eyes. "I love it!"

"It's perfect," Philippe said, pressing a kiss to Gabriella's hair. "What better than a Cinderella theme for our daughter's room?"

Eventually, we ate our dinner together, while we all took turns tossing around silly and outlandish ideas for baby girl names.

CHAPTER FOUR

On Saturday, the River Road Garden Center was holding a big Halloween/Harvest event. Not only was Saturday typically the busiest day of the week, retail-wise for them—it was only two weeks before Halloween, meaning the garden center would be packed with families. There'd be tons of kids running through the hay bale maze, searching for pumpkins to make into the perfect jack-o'-lanterns, and of course all of their parents who would be doing the shopping.

With that thought in mind, I'd loaded up a cardboard box with the new celestial molded soaps, a miniature wooden crate that held pumpkin spice lip balms, a sandwich baggie full of lip balm testers, and dozens of soap sample give-a-ways.

The samples were from my surplus soaps that I'd cut into four sections. To make them prettier, I'd sat up for hours and had tied raffia bows and tags, with the name of the soap and listed ingredients, to every single sample. I'd probably still be at it, if Drusilla, hadn't pitched in and given me a hand. Between the two of us we'd finished up around one o'clock in the morning.

I arrived at the garden center at 7:45am. Some of the staff were already at work setting out fresh corn stalk bundles for folks to purchase and of course, even more pumpkins on hay bales in front of the store. I pulled slowly to the back where the employees parked and managed to squeeze my truck into the last spot. Before I hopped out, I did one final check of my appearance in the rearview mirror.

My pale pink scoop-neck t-shirt actually complimented my hair. You'd be surprised how hard it was to find a shade of pink that didn't clash. I'd opted for casual today and wore dark jeans with my favorite black pleather jacket and ankle high, low heel boots.

Today I'd kept my makeup more subdued

than usual with taupe eye shadow and charcoal liner to accent my green eyes. I'd switched the thin silver nose ring to a tiny diamond stud. The rest of my jewelry was simple: a shimmery crescent moon pendant and small dangling lunar earrings that matched.

"Here we go." I fluffed up my blonde and pink bob and climbed out of the truck. I went around to the passenger side, pulled out the big box of supplies and samples and shut the door with my elbow.

I went directly to the back door and met Max as he exited. "Morning!" I called out.

"Morning, glory." He stopped and pressed a brotherly kiss to my cheek.

"Ready for today?" I asked.

"Two weeks before Halloween is always the busiest day for pumpkin sales," Max said. "Weather forecast is clear, cool and dry. We're going to be packed."

"I saw in the paper that you have face painting and pony rides advertised for today."

"Yeah, Nicole had this idea to make it more like a festival. It's going to be a zoo. Literally."

"I'm sure Nicole can keep everything

organized," I said.

"No, there's supposed to be a petting zoo... rabbits, goats, a pony, that sort of thing. But the guy is running late and Nicole is pissed." Max shook his head. "God help anyone who screws up her work schedule."

"I see." I bit down on the inside of my lip as not to laugh. I wished him good luck and let myself in the back door.

Nicole was standing behind the front counter, counting the drawer down. "Hi Cammy." She flashed me a smile and kept on working.

"In case you didn't get my email, here's the new items I'm bringing in," I said, pulling a paper from my pocket and handing her a list of the new items on my inventory.

Nicole nodded. "Got the email and added them into the system early this morning."

"You make my organized Virgo soul very happy," I said, tucking the list away.

"I'm an Aries," Nicole said. "I am happiest when things run smoothly."

I eyeballed the brunette standing behind the counter. Today she was wearing a denim shirt with the garden center logo embroidered on it.

The shirt was open and worn like a jacket, over a bright orange t-shirt. Her khakis were sturdy and spotless, and tiny enameled jack-o'-lantern earrings swung cheerfully from her ears.

"An Aries, eh?" I tilted my head as I considered what her astrological sign said about her. "A fire sign. Folks think you're hard-headed or bossy, but in reality you're an energetic worker and have zero patience for anything that moves or operates too slowly."

"Yes." She nodded. "Like the old check-out system Max had in place that should have been relegated to the Stone Age. I took that over this summer and pulled him into the twenty-first century." She checked her watch. "Damn it, the petting zoo people are running way behind schedule."

"Turtle slow, eh?" I couldn't help but tease her.

She gave me a withering look, and the store phone rang. Nicole pounced. "River Road Garden Center," she said into the phone. "How much later?"

I shifted the box to my hip and watched Nicole. A college aged student entered the back door, lifted a hand to Nicole in greeting, and hauled a rolling makeup case with her.

"We advertised for pony rides, and a petting zoo for the children today." Nicole's voice was silky smooth with a layer of steel beneath. "You were scheduled to start at nine o'clock this morning. I suggest you *be* on time, if you want to participate in this event in the future."

"Problem?" I asked after she hung up.

"Nothing I can't handle." She flashed a determined smile and went to go speak to the face painter.

I carried the box over to my booth. Someone had tucked a chair in behind the display table for me, should I wish to sit. I set the box on the chair and swiftly checked my table. A few things were out of place, so I shrugged off my jacket and put things back in order. Taking a quick visual inventory, I saw that a couple bars of soap had sold, but other than that...nothing.

"Well that's why I'm here today," I reminded myself. "To drum up some business."

I shifted the potpourri basket, making some room on the display table, and added in a few of the celestial molded soaps and the wooden box holding the pumpkin lip balm. I lifted the long-handled basket out of the box I'd brought in and quickly filled it with the tagged soap samples and the baggie of pumpkin lip balm testers I'd marked as 'Samples.' Once I had the basket organized, I slid the cardboard box under my table.

A vendor from the nearby apple orchard had set up a card table full of jars of apple butter, pumpkin butter, and local honey. The woman told me that depending on how they did today, they might rent a retail booth space from Max and Nicole like I was doing.

Nicole unlocked the doors at nine, and within minutes cars were pulling into the garden center. I hooked the sample basket over my arm and got ready to rock and roll.

Within an hour I had handed out several samples, sold a jar of lotion, two bath bombs, and a bar of soap. I'd given a tester of the pumpkin lip balm to the face painter and the apple butter lady. As I'd hoped, they were both talking me up to the customers.

By noon the garden center was rocking, and children stood in line to have their faces painted. I spotted a familiar young blonde boy. Jaime was dancing in place and holding the hand of a full figured, older woman. He was looking around with curiosity, and when he spotted me he started to grin.

"Hello, Jaime." I waved at him.

"Hi Cammy!" He tugged on the woman's fingers. "Grandma, this is Cammy. Told you she had pink hair."

"Hello," I smiled at Jaime's grandmother. "I'm Camilla Midnight."

"Oh, you're the one." She smiled down at her grandson. "I'm Jenna," she said, introducing herself.

That family certainly has a thing for names that begin with a J, I thought.

Jenna wore a black Halloween t-shirt featuring a cat wearing a Witch's hat. Behind stylish, wire rimmed glasses I noticed she had the same blue eyes as her son and grandson.

"It's nice to meet you," I said.

"What's in the basket, Camilla?" Jenna wanted to know.

"A few samples of my wares." I winked at her. I pulled a mini bar out. "This is my handmade, honey oatmeal soap."

Jenna pulled her hand back. "Does that contain nuts? Jaime has a severe peanut allergy."

"No ma'am, it does not." I flipped the tag over. "All the ingredients are listed, and the soaps are completely nut free."

"I love a nice, handmade soap," Jenna said, and gave the sample a good sniff. "Smart to list the ingredients for folks with allergies."

It was Jaime's turn and he hopped up on the stool and told the face painter he wanted a 'scary pumpkin' painted on his face. "Right here," he said, pointing to his right cheek.

"James Alexander," Jenna said in a stern tone of voice. "I'm going to step over here with Camilla to see her soaps."

"Okay, Grandma." Jaime seemed unfazed by the use of his full name.

Jenna moved with me over to my booth, but stayed where she could keep Jaime in her line of sight.

I smiled as she perused the display. "There is coconut oil in my lip balms, and cocoa butter in some of my lotions and soaps," I explained.

"Would that cause any problems with his allergies?"

"No. Coconut and chocolate won't bother him...but the peanut allergy makes Halloween a real challenge, let me tell you." Jenna bent over and sniffed at the autumn mix of potpourri. "Oh, now that's lovely."

"Do you like pumpkin spice?" I asked.

Jenna picked up a bag of the potpourri. "You bet I do. It's wonderfully cozy at this time of year."

I plucked a lip balm tester out of my basket and pulled the cap off the tube. "Try this seasonal lip balm that I make. It's pumpkin spice flavored."

Jenna accepted the sample, gave it a sniff. "What's in this?"

"Coconut oil, beeswax, cocoa butter, a little pumpkin pie spice, vanilla, and pumpkin puree."

"Real pumpkin?" Jenna laughed, and rolled some on. She pressed her lips together and then her eyes lit up as she tasted it. "Oh my. How much?" she wanted to know.

I handed her the cap. "This is a tester. It's

free."

As we spoke, a few other women and a teenage girl wandered over and began to check out the display.

"Mom!" the teen said excitedly. "She has bath bombs!" The girl hunkered down and began going through the varieties.

"I'm going to need a shopping basket," Jenna predicted. "I think I'm going to want a few of everything."

On cue, Nicole appeared with an apple basket. "Here you go, Jenna."

Jenna checked over her shoulder to see if Jaime was still having his face painted, and she took the basket and loaded up. Besides the autumn potpourri, Jenna picked up two more bars of the honey oatmeal soap, a full-size tube of the pumpkin lip balm, and a jar of shaving soap for her husband.

While Nicole handed out apple baskets to the other shoppers, I tried to act casual, but I was thrilled to my toes. The teenage girl had selected a bath bomb in every color and was asking questions about them.

"No," I assured her. "The bath bombs won't

turn your skin colors."

Jaime came skipping over, his face freshly painted. "Grandma, look!"

Jenna leaned over, took Jaime's chin in her hand and carefully studied the artwork. "That is, without a doubt, the best jack-o'-lantern I've ever seen painted on anyone's face," she said seriously.

Jaime giggled. Then he spotted her basket. "Whatcha buying, Grandma?"

"Some soaps, and smell good things." She patted his head.

"Can I have something?" Jaime wanted to know.

I fished a sample of the honey oatmeal soap out of my sample basket. "You can use this the next time you take a bath."

"What is it?" Jaime sniffed the bar.

"It's soap. Don't eat it," I said, anticipating him

"It smells like oatmeal cookies," Jaime decided.

"It's soap," I said firmly. "It will make your dry skin less itchy."

"How did you know he has dry skin?" Jenna

asked.

Before I could answer, Nicole came by with a tray of samples of the apple butter in tiny cups. "Would anyone like to try the apple butter? It's from the local orchard, nut free, and organic."

Jenna laid a hand on her ample bosom. "Girl, I never refuse anything sweet."

Nicole passed out the apple butter, and I handed out more free samples of soap. The day was loud, busy and fun. By the time seven o'clock rolled around, my table was almost empty. I'd run out of the free samples by three o'clock. The bath bombs were all but gone, and the lip balm, in every flavor, was sold out.

The display I'd worked so hard on was decimated. I was down to a couple of bars of soap, two bottles of shampoo, a lone bottle of lotion, a single jar of shaving soap, and the winter mix of the potpourri...and that was it. I was thrilled.

The lady selling apple butter was also pleased with her sales, and I bought a jar of local honey from her for my next batch of honey oatmeal soap. *Good god,* I realized as I sat down behind the table. *In order to fully restock my supplies I was going to have to work some crazy long hours over the next week.* I'd done fairly well at the Farmer's Market this summer, and I did have more soaps and lotions stored at the farmhouse, but today had been amazing. I went over the notes I'd taken on people's comments, and what items had sold out first, and tried to come up with a schedule and a work list of what items to begin with, allowing for curing time and so forth.

"I see my mom wasn't kidding," said a male voice.

I snapped my head up from my list and discovered Jacob, the sexy landscaper, standing in front of my table. "Hello." I smiled up at him. *He certainly was yummy,* I thought as my heart gave a happy flutter. He was much taller than me, and I had to tip my head back to meet his eyes.

"She said your stuff had been selling like hotcakes." Jacob tucked his hands in his front pockets. "I was hoping to get some lip balm from you. Max swears by it."

"I'll be making more," I said, studying his

face and the scruff that was on his jawline. "Here." I stood and handed him the last jar of shaving soap. "Try this the next time you shave."

Jacob popped the lid off the jar and sniffed. "Smells good," he said, and stepped a tad closer. His eyes met mine, and slowly, he smiled. "What's that scent?"

"Frankincense." I smiled back, recognizing his subtle flirtation. "Shaving soaps allow for a closer shave, and are more environmentally friendly than store-bought shaving cream."

"No aerosol," Jacob said, and angled his body even closer to mine.

"Right." I studied his blue eyes. "Also, the lanolin in the soap will keep your skin healthier." Testing, I lifted a hand to his jaw and trailed a finger over the stubble. "Plus, if you nick yourself, it will speed up healing."

He caught my fingers with one hand and gave them a soft squeeze. "How about the frankincense?" His voice was low and husky.

We stood close together, and my heart began to beat faster in reaction as Jacob's eyes traveled down and then slowly back up to my face. It made me imagine him as a lover, and wondering, I yearned.

"And the frankincense?" he reminded me with a smile.

"The essential oil has a high spiritual vibration," my answer was automatic. "It's often used for protection and good luck."

His smile was replaced by a slight frown. Dropping my hand, Jacob stepped back, and narrowed his eyes in consideration. "So, you're really into all of that?" He made a waving motion as if to encompass my whole person. His energy had suddenly shifted. I could feel it. What had started out as a flirtatious vibe had morphed into slight condescension.

"You literally gestured to all of me." I chuckled in an attempt to lighten the mood. "What do you mean by *all of that*?"

"The whole witchy thing." Jacob closed the lid on the shaving soap and set the jar down. "Or aesthetic—I guess you'd call it."

I fell back on my best socially acceptable defense, light sarcasm. "Well, well..." I raised an eyebrow. "You used the word 'aesthetic' in a sentence. I'm *very* impressed at the depth of your vocabulary skills."

Jacob smiled at my snarkiness. "Just because I plant trees for a living doesn't mean I'm stupid," he said. "And you didn't answer my question."

I picked up my jacket and shrugged it on. "And what exactly was the question?"

"Are you into the whole Witch thing?"

"Witch thing?" I narrowed my eyes at how glibly he'd said that.

"Yeah, you know. I figured with Halloween coming up, it's a good hook."

"A good hook?" I sputtered. I wasn't often at a lack of words, but at that moment I'd been reduced to two or three word replies.

Jacob tucked his hands back in his pockets. "Sure, I bet the idea that you might actually *be* a Witch helps increase the sales of your soaps and..." He gestured to the sign. "Potions."

Now, I was offended. "*Excuse me?*"

"Oh relax, Camilla." Jacob tried a smile. "I'm not giving you grief about your little hobby."

Forget offended. Now I was going straight towards pissed. "You appear to be laboring under a misassumption." I said, slowly and deliberately. "Magick isn't a hobby."

Jacob tipped his head to one side. "Then what is it?"

"That's a complicated answer, Jacob." Taking a deep breath, I reminded myself that losing my temper with an employee of the garden center wasn't good for my booth's future. I considered my options and decided to proceed with care. "It would be easier to tell you what magick *isn't*," I finally said.

"Okay," he said. "What isn't it?

Deliberately, I met his eyes. "Magick doesn't coerce, force, or control."

"So it's not about power."

"Power over another? No. It shouldn't be," I explained quietly. "At its best, magick is a type of harmony. A blending of personal power," I placed a hand over my own heart. "Or personal energy—you might say—combined with the energies of nature, in order to create a positive change."

Jacob stared at me, the expression in his blue eyes was plainly disbelieving.

"Let me put this in terms you'll be more

familiar with," I said, hooking the sample basket over one arm. "You plant trees and perennials with an eye to the future, right? To change a landscape for the better?"

"Yes." Jacob nodded.

"I imagine the garden design works better when you work *with* the features that are already in play, as opposed to working against them or trying to introduce a plant that isn't suited to the local environment."

"That's true."

"You use the creativity and knowledge that you have, and select the plants that will be the most complimentary for the climate and sun exposure. You craft something beautiful out of nothing—using your own energy and talents. It takes a certain type of magick to make a lasting change for the better to the landscape."

Jacob stood staring at me for a moment. "That's a lot deeper than I would have expected coming from someone who looks like you."

"Meaning what, exactly?"

"You know..." He shrugged. "The whole artsy, rocker-chick vibe."

"Don't let the pink hair fool you, Jacob," I

warned, mentally upgrading him from 'condescending jerk' to 'narrow-minded asshole'. It had been a long, long time since anyone had made me this angry. Still, I fought not to let it show.

"My mom always said the Midnight women were different," Jacob said. "Wiser," he continued, blissfully unaware of how tightly I was holding onto my temper. "Yeah, wiser... more intuitive."

I forced myself to lower my shoulders. I'd bunched them up defensively tight while we'd been talking. "Your mother seems like a smart woman." *Unlike her son.*

"How much for the shaving soap?"

His question caught me off guard. The last thing I'd expected after our exchange was for him to purchase something. I made an effort to keep my tone light. "Feeling brave enough to try it, are you?"

"Sure, why not?" Jacob chuckled and picked up the jar again. "I don't see any eye of newt listed on the ingredients tag." He made a show of reading it. "How much?"

He honestly thought he was being funny, I

realized. "Ten dollars," I said, holding onto my temper by my fingernails. "I'm sure Nicole will be happy to ring you up."

"Do I get an employee discount?" he asked cheerfully.

I tucked my lists in my empty sample basket. "You'll have to ask Nicole." I picked up my purse and sailed past him. "Excuse me."

I waved to Nicole and headed for the back door. Anger was radiating off me in waves and I fought to keep my energy under control before it accidentally caused a problem. As I walked to the parking lot the security lights mounted on the back of the building flickered.

"Shit," I said under my breath. I increased my pace, determined to get out of there before I blew up something electrical.

I opened the truck's door, tossed in the basket and purse, and jumped in the cab. I had barely started the engine when Jacob's handsome face appeared in my driver's side window.

"Hey." He tapped on the glass.

I grit my teeth and rolled down the window. "Yes?"

"I'm sorry if I offended you." He tried a

smile. "I wasn't trying to."

"Yet you succeeded, beautifully," I said through clenched teeth.

He leaned in closer through the open window. "So, you dress like a rocker chick, encourage folks to think you're a Witch...But yet, you have no sense of humor, is that it?"

I'd never have someone flirt *and* simultaneously make fun of me before. My anger spiked and the security lights went out with a loud sizzle and pop.

Jacob jumped back swinging his gaze toward the security lights. "What the hell?"

I gripped the steering wheel tighter and fought silently for control.

He stared at me with very wide eyes. "You're not going to turn me into a frog are you?"

"Jacob, I promise you..." I flashed him a wicked smile. "I can come up with something *much* more creative." Gunning the engine, I backed out of the parking spot with a small spray of gravel.

CHAPTER FIVE

I did my best to put the incident with Jacob out of my mind. There was a lot of work to do and I shook off any thoughts of revenge, telling myself he wasn't worth my time. Referring to my notes and work lists, I spent the next week making soaps, shampoo, lotions, lip balms, and bath bombs. The family kitchen resembled the laboratory of a mad scientist after a few days. The table in the laundry room was full, and I had an extra six-foot work table set up temporarily in the kitchen where I stored more soaps, allowing them to set up and harden.

Thankfully, Gran pitched in and helped me, and young Brooke James came over on Friday evening while her guardian, Garrett Rivers, and my sister Drusilla, had a date night. The eleven-year-old was more than happy to help me package everything up.

I'd sprung for pizza and after a while the two of us took a break, sitting on the back porch devouring the mushroom and pepperoni pie, while Brooke chugged her contraband soda.

"You won't tell Garrett that I drank soda, will you?" Brooke asked.

"Not if you don't tell Gran that the burn mark on the kitchen table is from me dropping a pot." I held out my fist for a knuckle bump.

Brooke pressed her knuckles to mine. "Done."

"I got your back, sister," I said seriously, and took a sip of my red wine.

"I got yours." Brooke slurped her soda and kicked back in the wrought iron chair.

I let my mind wander and realized that I was looking forward to actually getting out of the house and going into Alton tomorrow to begin my research on the history of the Marquette mansion and the family who'd lived there in the 1840's. Philippe had asked me to drop by for dinner afterwards. He wanted to give me some information his grandfather had recently sent to help with the research.

The tortoiseshell cat the family had adopted wandered over and leaned against my ankles. "Hi Mama Cat." I gave her an ear rub and the cat purred loudly.

"Hey, Cammy?" Brooke asked.

"Yeah?"

"Do you think maybe you could teach me magick?" Brooke's voice was hesitant. "I've been thinking about it for a long time...I figured you'd be the best person to ask."

I turned to regard her as she sat in profile staring across the gardens. "Why do you want to learn magick, Brooke?"

"Mom always told me stories when I was little about how the Rivers family—her family —was descended from a water spirit. A goddess of the water named Melusine. It's why she named me Brooke."

"I've seen the family crest Garrett has displayed at your house."

Brooke nodded. "Yeah, the mermaid with two tails. I mean how cool is that?"

"It's very cool," I agreed. "What was your mother's full name?"

"Melissa Lena Rivers," she said. "Mom said that her dad named her after the goddess."

"And her father's first name was?"

Brooke frowned. "Dylan. With a Y. He died before I was born, but I checked that spelling online. The website said it was Welsh, and that his name meant 'son of the sea'."

Clever girl, I thought. "You've been busy." I smiled at her and wondered if she was indeed aligned to the element of water, as her ancestors believed.

"Well, it got me to thinking...and I researched other water goddesses online. I started to check out more magick stuff and spells on the internet." Brooke shrugged. "But that mostly seemed like bullshit."

My lips twitched at her swearing. "You'd be correct about the bullshit on the internet," I answered solemnly. "But why do you *really* want to learn magick?"

Brooke faced me, and her bottom lip trembled. "I never told anyone, because it scared me too much." She nervously licked her lips. "Last spring at school, when those girls cornered me in the bathroom. After they knocked me down, and I landed on my arm funny, all the faucets in the bathroom sinks came on by themselves. While they were laughing at me, the water went everywhere and made the floor slippery. I tried to stand up, and I fell again and hit my face on the sink. The water wouldn't turn off, no matter what they did, and after I hit Clementine with my backpack, they got scared and ran away. Then I ran out of school and came here to hide."

"Which is when Dru found you." I sighed. "Has this problem with water ever happened to you before or since?" I asked gently.

"We have a lot of problems with the plumbing at the house." Brooke hunched her shoulders. The toilets overflow and the water comes on by itself. The plumber is always working on it."

"And you thought what happened at school was because of magick?"

"I wondered," she said. "I thought maybe I could use magick to bring my mom and dad back."

I reached out instantly to the girl. She'd been through so much. "Oh, sweetie I'm sorry." I gave her hand a squeeze. "Magick doesn't work like that."

"I figured that out for myself." Brooke tossed her long red braid over her shoulder. "But Drusilla believes in faeries, and I've seen the way the plants and animals are when she works in the gardens. The plants reach out for her, and they sort of talk to her. And then there's Gran," she said of my grandmother. "She knows *everything*. Like even before the phone rings. The other day she told me to go answer the kitchen phone, and then it rang. That phone doesn't even have Caller ID."

I glanced through the window at the old land line rotary phone that still hung on the kitchen wall.

Brooke took a deep breath and continued. "I know that Ella did something to my wrist after I broke it. Before Dru got me to the hospital, Ella held her hand over my wrist and said a sort of rhyming poem in the car...and afterwards it didn't hurt as much."

"I see." I sat back. The girl had been much more aware of my family's practices than I'd ever given her credit for.

Brooke's hydrangea blue eyes searched mine. "I figured that she worked a spell on me."

I nodded. "A healing spell, most likely."

Brooke blinked. "It's true then."

"Yes," I said simply.

"People in the village talk about the daughters of Midnight. I heard one lady say you were wise women. What does that mean?"

"The women of my family are descended from healers and herbalists. The term 'wise woman' is an old one."

"I read about that," Brooke said. "This one site said that the word *Wicca* means wise. Is this magick that you do like Wicca?"

I smiled. "Yes and no. The members of my family have never used that modern term. They quietly practice the old ways, and have always referred to themselves as wise women, or in some cases, cunning men."

"So a boy could do this too, if he wanted."

"Of course."

She seemed to think that over. "Cool. Can you teach me?"

"There is a lot to learn," I warned her. "This isn't an 'I read one book and now I'm done' type of scenario, Brooke. You will never truly stop studying or learning when it comes to magick."

Brooke's eyes were intense. "I'm not afraid to learn."

I recognized the stubborn set of her jaw. I'd been much the same once. Determined to push the envelope and willing to learn more. "I'll tell you what," I said. "If Garrett gives his permission, then yes, I will." I promised.

"And if he won't?"

"Then you'll have to wait a few years. When you become eighteen if you still would like to learn, I'll teach you then."

"Okay." Brooke picked up another piece of pizza. "I wish you could teach me something now."

I considered the dark gardens. Gran was out for the evening and no one would disturb us. "Come with me," I said, and stepped off the back porch and into the grass. "I want to test a theory."

Brooke jumped off the porch and raced to follow me. "Where are we going? What are we going to do?"

I held out my hand for the girl. "You'll see."

She put her hand in mine and we walked around the garden hose Dru had left stretched across the grass, and over to the gazebo. The waning moon was rising in the eastern sky, and a kicky October breeze sent a few oak leaves scuttling across the concrete floor of the gazebo. I walked with her to the center of the gazebo and positioned her so we stood facing each other.

"Hold your hands up," I directed. "With our palms pressing together."

Silently, Brooke pressed her hands to mine.

"Now I want you to take a deep breath," I said. "Hold it for a count of four and then slowly blow it out..." I took the girl through the basics of grounding and centering, and when I felt she was ready, I moved on to a call to the elements.

I called to earth first, and told Brooke to close her eyes and visualize the element of earth all around her. From the flowers in the garden to the oak tree in the yard. I encouraged her to feel the ground under her feet, strong and supportive. "Hail to the element of earth," I said, and had Brooke repeat the words after me. I watched, but saw no changes or manifestations of any kind that would indicate a connection to the element of earth.

Next, I moved to the element of air. I took her through the steps again and had her echo my words back to me.

"Hail to the element of air," Brooke said, and as soon as she uttered the words, the light breeze shifted, and a gust of wind whipped through the yard from the east. It sent my hair billowing around my face, and even more leaves tumbling across the gazebo floor.

Brooke's eyes popped wide. "What's happening?" she asked.

I smiled at her and tossed the hair out of my eyes. "Seems you are aligned to the element of air."

"I am?" Her voice was high with wonder.

"Element of air, we thank you. Depart in peace." I squeezed Brooke's fingers. "Say it with me." Together we said the words, and on the third repetition the wind from the eastern quarter suddenly stopped.

"Oh wow," Brooke whispered.

"Let's move on to the next element," I suggested. The element of fire was a bust. There was no discernable change in temperature, or light. I planted my feet and psyched myself up and moved on to the final element.

"What's next?" Brooke asked.

"The element of water," I said. "We're about to find out if the stories your mother told you are true." I linked fingers with her. "Now, no matter what happens, stay linked with me."

"Okay." Brooke's voice sounded very young all of a sudden.

"Are you ready?"

Brooke squeezed my hands. "Let's do it."

I grinned, and called to the element of water. I told Brooke to close her eyes and visualize the element of water all around her. From the rivers flowing past the village, to the night time dew that formed on the grass, and the rain that fell from the sky. "Hail to the element of water," I said, and Brooke chimed in.

The air went heavy, and the humidity increased immediately. A hush fell over the yard, and Brooke opened one eye. "Is anything happening?" she whispered. "The air feels funny."

"It's heavier, from the humidity—the water content has increased."

"I feel something." She began to tremble. "In the center of my chest. It's sort of tight."

"Let it go," I said. "Direct it. Aim it up and out."

"I'm trying." Brooke shuddered and her chin dropped on to her chest.

"Brooke!" I called her name urgently, but she didn't respond. "Call on the goddess of your ancestors. Call on Melusine."

Brooke's head rose slowly, and I saw that her eyes had shifted to a bright, preternatural shade of blue. "Melusine, please hear me," she said.

"I've got you," I told the girl, tightening my grip. "Call her again."

Brooke bore down and called out again.

I heard the hiss first, and I snapped my head around at the sound. The spray hit me in the face and I ducked. The garden hose that had been left stretched out across the lawn appeared to have sprung dozens of leaks. Little streams of water were shooting up all over the place.

The spray of water got Brooke squarely in the center of the chest. She jumped. "What's happening?"

"The element answered your call." I started to laugh. "The goddess Melusine heard you."

"Maybe the water was left on, and the hose sprang a leak." Brooke frowned.

"Let's go check!" I tugged her with me and we raced hand-in-hand through the spraying water and toward the house. I tightened the spigot with a quick twist. The water was off—yet water continued to blast incxplicably out of the holes in the hose.

"Did I do all of this?" Brooke sounded thrilled and terrified at the same time.

While Brooke stood there gaping, a splashing sound had me glancing to my right and I noticed that the water in the concrete bird bath was sloshing back and forth. "Okay, honey let's shut all this down."

"How?" Brooke wanted to know.

I took both of her hands in mine again. "Goddess Melusine, we thank you for your presence," I chanted. "Element of water, we release you. Depart in peace. Hail and farewell."

On the second repetition Brooke joined in. By the third she was standing strong and speaking clearly. As we finished up the third repetition the spray of water began to peter out. The waves in the bird bath slowly dissipated.

The typical night time noises returned. I nudged Brooke to sit on the wet grass and talked her through grounding her energy again. When we were finished I patted her on the head. "I'd say the stories your mother told you are true."

"I'm like Percy Jackson or something," Brooke said. Her mouth worked a few times. "Holy crap."

"Not quite. Percy was the fictional son of the Greek god Poseidon," I pointed out. "You're a descendant of Melusine—and you have a *definite* connection to the element of water, and also to air."

"What does that mean?" Brooke asked.

"It means whether Garrett likes it or not, we need to start training you right away, before this elemental ability gets any more out of hand."

"Will he be mad at me?"

I passed my hand over her bright red hair. "It's his heritage as well. I'll talk to him, don't you worry."

"I'm starving!" Brooke jumped to her feet, took a step, and swayed.

"Okay, my young apprentice." I hooked an arm around her waist to help her walk. "Let's start with the basics. Magick costs physical energy, and you just used a lot."

"Like a cell phone that's battery drained?"

"Sort of." I tugged her back to the porch and sat her down. I handed her the soda. "You need to refuel and rest. Sugar will help. So, bottom's up."

Brooke chugged her soda and burped loudly after she finished. She began to giggle. "I feel funny!"

"You're punch-drunk from the magick," I said, noting her neon blue eye color had yet to fade. "It'll pass. Let's get some food into you, so you can reconnect firmly to the physical plane."

"Okay." She swayed in her seat, grabbed a piece of pizza, and bit in.

"Now you see what *I* had to deal with when

you were younger." My grandmother's stern voice came from the kitchen door.

"Gran." I saw her and cringed. "I can explain."

"No need." She shook her head. "I've been watching since you took her over to the gazebo."

"Hi Gran!" Brooke beamed at my grandmother. "Guess what?" she said from around a mouth full of pizza. "I have magick!"

My grandmother caught her chin and leaned over to examine Brooke's face. "Drusilla told me that Garrett's eyes get like this occasionally."

"What do you mean?" Brooke asked, finishing her slice of pizza.

Gran patted her cheek. "Nothing for you to worry about, sweetie."

"I made the hose blow up!" Brooke said. "And the water in the birdbath sloshed all around."

"The kid's a natural," I said proudly.

"I'm a natural," Brooke repeated. With a sigh, she leaned back in the café chair, shut her eyes, and dropped off.

Gran rolled her eyes as Brooke began to snore softly. "Well, Camilla Jane, you can haul 'the natural' inside and put her on the couch so she can sleep this off."

"Yes ma'am." I tried to sound contrite, but some laughter bubbled out.

Gran scowled. "And then you can explain to Drusilla about her hose being ruined, clean up this pizza party, *and* clear away the mess you made in the kitchen."

"Have I told you lately how much I love you, Gran?" I grinned at the woman who'd raised me.

Gran's lips twitched. "Don't try and sweet talk your way out of this, young lady."

Gran held the door open for me. With no other options, I tugged Brooke over my shoulder from the chair. I straightened slowly with her in a fireman's carry and hauled the girl inside.

***

The talk with Garrett went easier than I'd imagined. Once I told him *all* the details from when Brooke had been bullied in the school bathroom, he put it together pretty quickly.

"Well," he said with a smirk towards Brooke as she slept on the couch, "that explains the mystery plumbing problems at the house."

"I knew it," Drusilla said, taking Garrett's left hand in her right. "I knew there was a real connection from Melusine to your family."

"You could have told me." Garrett smiled down at my sister.

Dru shrugged. "I didn't want to frighten you."

Garrett seemed to think it over. "Maybe this explains why I've never been comfortable living somewhere unless there is a body of water nearby..."

"Precisely." Gran nodded in agreement.

I spoke up. "I'd like the opportunity to work with her Garrett, with your permission of course."

Garrett looked to my sister. "What do you think, Drusilla?"

Dru gave his hand a squeeze. "I think that would be your wisest course of action. We *all* will work with her."

"Is this a wise woman thing?" Garrett asked us.

"Yes," Gran, Dru, and I all said together.

"Well then, I'm going to leave this in your hands." Garrett smiled. "You're the experts. But please keep me in the loop on her training or any other 'talents' that might pop up."

"Of course we will," Drusilla assured him.

Garrett blew out a long breath. "And to think I wanted a quiet, normal, ordinary life when I moved here."

"Too late now." Dru gave him a kiss on the lips. "Besides, being ordinary is immensely overrated."

The ease with which Garrett had accepted our heritage had my heart simply melting. I couldn't help but smile at the couple. My intuition suddenly kicked in and the psychic information that popped into my head was coming out of my mouth before I could stop it. "Drusilla Anne." I stared at her. "The man proposed...and you didn't tell us *immediately*?"

Dru hissed. "Damn it, Camilla Jane." She pulled her left hand from her pocket. "I wanted to surprise the family when we were all together."

"I want to see the ring!" Gran demanded with a laugh, while Dru obligingly held out her hand.

I echoed the sentiment and took Dru's hand, admiring the pretty engagement ring. A central blue sapphire was flanked by two diamonds and set on a platinum band. It was elegant and lovely, not unlike my sister. "Congratulations." I gave her a hug and then Garrett one.

After the congratulatory hugs and kisses were finished, Garrett went over to his ward with Drusilla. He passed a hand over the girl's red hair. "Brooke," he said. "You're going to want to wake up."

Brooke sat up from the center of the couch and rubbed her eyes. She spotted Garrett and Drusilla standing together and smiled sleepily. "Did she like the ring we picked out?" Brooke asked Garrett, around a yawn.

"She did," Garrett said, and grinned down at the girl.

"Okay, good." Brooke yawned again. "Please hurry up and marry him Dru."

I smiled. "Brooke, they'll need *some* time to plan."

Drusilla smiled at Garrett. "Cammy is right. I'm going to want a formal wedding, and that takes time to organize."

Garrett kissed the knuckles above her engagement ring. "You want a fancy wedding? I can arrange that," he said.

"Lovely." Gran nodded her head in agreement.

"Can I be a bridesmaid?" Brooke asked.

Drusilla sat beside the girl and slipped an arm around her. "I think you'll have to be our maid of honor."

"That's cool," Brooke said, leaning against Dru. "Afterwards, I want you two guys to officially become my parents. Maybe you could *both* adopt me..."

Garrett nodded and took a seat on Brooke's other side. "We could do that."

"Then I'd be your daughter." Brooke said, and her voice slurred a little.

Drusilla's eyes immediately began to fill. "I'd like that very much." She dropped a kiss on the girl's forehead. "In fact, I'd *love* it."

Brooke's eyes began to drift shut. "Dru, you'd be a really cool mom..." She trailed off.

"Can we talk about it more in the morning?" she asked them.

Garrett gave her shoulders a squeeze. "Of course we can."

"Okay." Brooke smiled, fell over on the pillows, and immediately started to snore.

CHAPTER SIX

Garrett and Drusilla went back to his house, taking the opportunity to celebrate their engagement in private. After they left, Brooke continued to sleep off the effects of her first controlled magick, and I stayed up working for most of the night. I managed to finish the packaging of all my new soaps, bath bombs, and lotions I'd made to restock my booth. Afterward, I finally cleaned up the kitchen as Gran had requested.

I managed to grab a quick nap, and at dawn I headed across the hall to the shower. I refueled with a few cups of very strong tea and did my hair and face. I took the time to make my bed, as I simply couldn't relax or get anything accomplished unless my personal space was tidy.

My bedroom was my haven. It was comforting and cozy with pale gray walls, a gray tufted headboard and white and gray patterned bed pillows. I'd added a splash of color with a blush pink comforter and a white pillow that featured a pink peony in full bloom. A set of four old botanical drawings of *Zephrine Drouhin* roses, pink peonies and various herbs in bloom were arranged on the wall above my bed. My furniture was all mismatched, and I liked it that way. The old vanity I'd inherited from my Gran I'd painted a soft pink, with black trim. I switched out the hardware to black, and Ella had helped me reupholster the padded seat in a black and white toile.

Tugging on a pair of dark jeans, I headed to my closet and paused in my bra and pants, trying to decide what top to wear. I needed to seem approachable while doing research. Even with degrees in history and historic preservation, I knew folks were more inclined to talk to you and share information if you didn't come across too strong or appear too gothic. With that in mind, I did my eyes in shades of green and charcoal, left the tiny diamond stud in place in my nose, and fluffed up my pink bob.

My bedroom door opened and I had to squelch down a laugh when Brooke came staggering in.

"Hey," the eleven-year-old mumbled, and went to throw herself—face down—on my freshly made bed.

I cringed at her flopping, and resigned myself to the fact that I would have to remake the bed. Selecting a thin, white, oversized sweater, I tossed it over my head and tugged it down. "How do you feel this morning?" I asked her.

"Bad." Brooke pushed herself up on her elbows. "I'm dizzy, my head hurts, plus it feels like it's way up here." She held a hand over her head to demonstrate.

"Magickal hangover," I explained. "The after effects of working a lot of magick. Do you remember Garrett and Drusilla talking to you last night?"

"Yeah," Brooke admitted with a gigantic yawn. "Did I ask them to adopt me last night?"

"You sure did," I said.

"I thought I remembered that." Brooke propped her chin on her hands. "Is Drusilla here, now?"

"No." I smiled. "They went back to Garrett's to celebrate their engagement in private,"

"Oh." Brooke stretched. "I guess they had sex, and stuff."

"I'd say that's a safe bet." I tried to keep a straight face. "Anyway, we did manage to talk to Garrett about your studies."

Now she rolled over to sit up. "You did?"

"Yes, we did." I selected a pair of low heeled black boots and sat at my vanity table chair to tug them on. "He's agreed to let us all work with you."

"Really?" Brooke shoved her hair out of her face.

"Really." I smiled at her. "I believe that Gran wants to have a talk with you this morning, she's probably waiting for you downstairs."

Brooke jumped off the bed and ran over to hug me. "Thanks Cammy!" She sped out of my room and clattered loudly down the stairs.

With a sigh I got up, straightened the

comforter, and re-arranged the pillows to their proper places. Satisfied that everything was tidy, I grabbed my pink pleather motorcycle jacket, slipped it on and headed out.

It didn't take me long to re-fill my booth at the garden center. It wasn't as full to bursting as it had been last week, but it was nicely stocked, completely organized, and ready for more customers. Nicole handed me an envelope with my sales from the previous weekend and when I checked the amount, I had to struggle to keep a neutral expression.

The amount was much larger than I'd hoped for. Even with the ten percent commission that the garden center deducted from my sales. I planned to reinvest all the profits into the business, and to order more supplies. I made a mental note to purchase several small baskets so I could make gift baskets to sell for the holidays.

I waved goodbye to Nicole and drove to the quaint museum in Ames Crossing. I truly didn't expect to find anything earth-shattering on the original Marquette family there, but still, I searched through the information that our museum had, hoping for any more material or photos of the mansion from back in its hey day. To my surprise there wasn't any. Nothing at all.

When I'd asked about additional photos of the house, I'd been given a cool stare and clipped response on limited funding. But it made me curious. *How could a local house owned by an influential family not have garnered a few more photos?*

I smiled at the suspicious volunteer and picked up a thin book on the founding family. After a quick glance, I discovered that it was mostly on the brothers they'd named our village after. One brother, Jonah Ames Sr., had owned the local stone quarry, and the second brother had been a railroad baron. I purchased the book anyway, and then drove over to Alton.

I struck gold with holiday baskets at a local craft store. I picked up a dozen and was delighted to get them on sale. I loaded them in the trunk and headed towards my next stop.

My goal was to check out the Alton Genealogy & Local History Library in the hopes that I'd find more information about the Marquettes, and I had a hunch if I dug deep enough, I might be able to uncover more details about the bride, Bridgette.

The library was lovely. I had a nice stack of books on the history of Jersey County and the railroad that had run through the village once upon a time. I'd even stumbled over line drawings of the old grain ports along the river's edge. While the reference books were not available to borrow, I was able to make copies. Digging out some change, I got to work.

Stacking up the last of my copied pages I started to go, and was hit with a strong tug at my midsection. Intrigued, I moved in the direction of that intuitive pull, and a glass-fronted case caught my eye. Wandering closer, I saw that it was filled with a genealogical display of a family that had lived in the area since pre-Civil War times. There was ephemera, photos, and a few framed drawings of one of the oldest limestone houses in Ames Crossing.

I scanned the pictures of a few members of the family who had served in Word War I and II, reading the caption beneath the soldier's names. Then the hair rose on the back of my neck.

The name of the family history on display in the case, was Ames.

Knowing there was no such thing as a random event, I took a deep breath and studied the exhibition more carefully. I pulled my cell phone from my pocket and took a few fast pictures of the display. There was a daguerreotype situated at the top. The image on the polished silver glass was of two women. Neither were smiling.

The women were quaffed and dressed in gowns typical of the 1800's. It was easy to see they'd been affluent because of the gowns, the hairstyle and the jewelry they were wearing. I slid my eyes to the neatly printed tag below the image and bobbled my phone.

The caption read: *Mary and Bridgette Ames. 1846.*

"There you are," I said.

There was a small newspaper clipping dated 1847 directly beneath. It was from an Alton newspaper, and the headline read: 'Bride Disappears: Foul Play Suspected'. The print was small and faded, and I had trouble reading it. Checking over my shoulder, I saw the coast was clear and took several more pictures of the two women, the caption beneath, the newspaper article, and finally a few more of the entire display of the Ames family.

I checked my phone and was satisfied with the images I'd captured. I'd only put the phone in my jacket pocket when a cheerful voice had me jolting.

"Can I help you, dear?"

I discovered an elderly woman wearing snazzy red glasses. Her nametag read *Francis*. "What can you tell me about this genealogical display?" I asked politely.

"Quite a bit. I did this presentation myself," she said proudly.

"It's wonderful." I nodded. "I'm very interested in your display. I'm from Ames Crossing, and am researching the genealogy of one of the local families."

"Which family?" she asked.

"The Marquettes."

She gave me a bland stare and I fought not to squirm. "I'd heard a descendant of the Marquette family had moved back to the area," she said. "Something about a winery and restoring the old mansion on the cliffs?"

"Yes ma'am," I said politely. "I'm working for Philippe Marquette." I tried not to feel badly about the fib. In a way, I was working for him.

Behind her bright red glasses, Francis narrowed her hazel eyes. "I suppose you are wanting to know about the scandal of the missing bride?" she asked.

"I heard about it only recently," I said. "According to Philippe, all the modern family knows is that she vanished shortly after the wedding."

"And so did her dowry," Francis said, wryly. "The disappearance of Bridgette Ames was a huge story in its day. The girl's older brother, Jonah Ames Jr., insisted that Pierre Michel Marquette had murdered the girl. Thrown poor Bridgette from the cliffs in a fit of rage, instead of remaining in an arranged marriage."

"Is that so?" I was surprised at her enthusiasm. You'd have thought she was speaking about current events, as passionate as she was.

"Now there were plenty of folks," Francis said, in a conspirator's whisper, "that thought the bride must have run off. Taken her dowry with her, hopped on a train and headed west to start a new life."

"Must have been some dowry," I said. "Does anyone know what her dowry actually consisted of?"

"Look here." Francis pointed to the image of the two sisters. "Bridgette, pictured on the right, was *wearing* some of her dowry."

I leaned my face close to the glass. "I see a bracelet, a necklace, maybe earrings."

"Earbobs, they called them back then," Francis corrected me. "It was an amethyst parure."

My breath whistled out. "A matched set of jewelry like that must have been worth a lot of money, even in the mid 1800's." *And the plot thickens...*I thought to myself. I slanted my gaze to Francis. "And they never found a trace of Bridgette or her jewelry?"

"No." Francis shook her head. "Of course, it was much easier to disappear and start a new life back then. But her brother Jonah searched for years. Supposedly he spent most of his fortune trying to find out what happened to his youngest sister. It was Jonah who was interviewed by the papers about his sister's disappearance, and you can see a snippet of that here." She tapped a coral fingernail on the glass.

"I wonder what happened to Bridgette?" I said, studying the picture of the serious young woman.

"There are those who say that she haunts the old, cursed mansion on the cliffs." Francis lowered her voice dramatically. "Forever walking, and searching for her jewels." Francis winked. "At least that's what I tell the local haunted tour attendees that come in here during weekends before Halloween..."

I grinned. Francis was making my day *and* confirming my theory of who the lady in white was at the mansion. "Would you be able to make a copy for me of those old newspaper clippings?" I asked politely.

Francis' hazel eyes twinkled. "I would," she said.

Francis was a gold mine of information. She'd given me a copy of the article on Bridgette's disappearance, and she'd also handed me another on the death of Pierre Michel Marquette. I sat at the library table, took notes on my conversation with Francis, and read over the small newspaper article about the death of Pierre Michel. It was very brief, but the most interesting part had been Mary Ames who'd been quoted as saying that with Pierre Michel's death, "Justice had finally been served."

There was no documentation of the 'curse' that she'd mentioned. But that didn't surprise me. *The curse was simply an embellishment,* I decided. Someone had cleverly added the curse to the story over the years, to make it sound more gothic and dramatic.

I thought over what I had learned as I drove back to the village and then up the steep road to Notch Cliff. I could hardly wait to tell Gabriella and Philippe about my chat with Francis at the library. I drove past the winery show room and the landscaping crew who were once again hard at work on the grounds surrounding the mansion.

I spotted Jacob almost immediately. "Why does he have to be so damn hot?" I muttered to myself as I drove closer. Jacob and his crew were busy building another retaining wall and spreading mulch around even more new trees. I figured they were trying to beat the frost, and although fall was an ideal time for planting, they were fast approaching the cut-off date.

I parked my car and climbed out. It was just my luck that Jacob decided to walk over to greet me. Taking a deep breath, I tucked the research folder under my arm, determined to be polite to the man, even if he was a narrow-minded jerk.

"Hello, Jacob." I lifted one hand in a casual wave, suddenly very glad I was dressed nicely.

"Hey, Cammy," he said.

"How goes the mulching?" I asked, watching as he maneuvered a full wheelbarrow to a new planting bed. It gave me a moment to appreciate the smooth flexing of the muscles in his arms.

Why are you admiring his arms? I scolded myself. *He might be attractive, but his attitude was anything but.*

"The landscaping is almost done." He set the wheelbarrow down, and the shovel slid off and landed on the ground. "What do you think of everything so far?" he asked, bending over in front of me to pick up the shovel.

I begrudgingly admired the view of his backside for a second and then shifted my gaze to the new stone retaining wall—before he turned around and caught me ogling him. I managed to give him a neutral smile. "Everything looks very nice to me."

"Very nice?" He scowled over my blasé answer for a moment.

"Yes," I said, gesturing to a nearby tree. "The *Cornus florida* should be beautiful next April when it blooms."

He blinked. "You know the botanical name of the dogwood tree?"

I spared him a small smile. "Of course I do. I'm a gardener and an herbalist, remember?"

"I think the *Quercus alba* Philippe chose was also a smart choice," he said casually.

Recognizing the challenge, I raised one eyebrow. "The white oak is an indigenous tree to Illinois. The autumn foliage will certainly be striking." I couldn't resist adding, "Did you know that in the language of flowers, the oak tree signifies hospitality, strength, and prosperity?"

Jacob studied me for a moment. "If you say so."

I was tempted to hit him with the shovel for being so thick-headed. Instead, I made an effort to project serenity as I spoke. "I do say so; just as the dogwood blossoms symbolize love and faithfulness."

His eyebrows went up. "So you're saying they chose the trees with those meanings in mind?"

"Gabriella would, absolutely." I allowed my lips to curve up in the slightest of smiles.

Jacob set the shovel aside. "So your whole family is into that stuff?"

I didn't deign to answer. Instead I met his eyes, held the gaze for a few moments, and said nothing.

"You're making me feel stupid for asking," he said.

"Then my work here is done." I gave him a cool nod. "If you'll excuse me." I began to walk past him.

"Camilla." He stopped me with a hand on my

arm.

I paused. "Yes?"

"I...I need to drop off the final invoice to Philippe. Do you know if he's at home?"

We both knew that wasn't what he intended to say. I looked from Jacob's hand up to his eyes. "I'm pretty sure he is," I said evenly. "They invited me for dinner."

"Mind if I walk with you?"

Yes I mind. "Not at all," I said instead, and was determined the man would have no reason to ever guess that my stomach was tied into knots. We fell in step together, and I tried to come up with something casually friendly to say. "How's Jaime doing?" I managed.

"He's with my mom this afternoon," Jacob said. "They're working on his Halloween costume."

We had only started down the brick pathway to the side entrance, and the door was flung open. It bounced off the side of the house, and a young woman ran outside.

"What in the world?" I had a split second to think she seemed familiar. "Donna Eckert, is that you?"

"Camilla? Oh thank god you're here!" She raced to me, flung her arms around my neck, and hung on.

"What's wrong, Donna?" I asked the girl I'd known back in high school. Gently, I pried her off me.

Donna pushed her mousey blonde hair out of her face. "I'm *never* going back in there." She shuddered.

"What happened?" Jacob demanded. "Are you alright?"

"I know they paid me to paint the mural in the nursery, but I—" The door banged shut behind her, and Donna scrambled farther away from the mansion with a terrified squeak.

I tipped my head up and scanned the exterior of the mansion. "I wonder..."

"I swear the house really is haunted!" Donna tried to pull me with her. "I'm never setting foot in that building again!"

I tried to calm her down, but she was having none of it. Donna took off at a dead run, and we watched her jog down the hill to the winery parking lot. She jumped in her car and took off with a loud squeal of tires.

"What in the hell could've happened in there to make her run like that?" Jacob said.

"I'm damn sure going to find out." I shoved open the side entrance door and hustled inside.

"Hang on a second." Jacob scrambled after me.

"Ella?" My voice echoed through the lobby and up the stairs. "Philippe?" I called out. "Are you guys home?" There was no answer, and the house was unnaturally still. I saw that Gabriella had started decorating inside the mansion as well. Pumpkins were stacked prettily on either side at the base of the stairs, and a fall garland and golden lights were wrapped around the ornate banister. But instead of being charmed by the decorations, I felt uneasy.

Jacob slipped in behind me and closed the door. "It doesn't feel right in here."

His statement had me frowning at him, especially considering how skeptical he was. "How *does* it make you feel?" I asked.

He rubbed his hand over the middle of his chest. "Sort of anxious," he admitted. "My chest feels tight."

Before I could comment, the sounds of

weeping drifted down from the floors above. "Do you hear that?" I whispered.

"Someone's crying," Jacob said.

My heart began to race. "That's not Gabriella."

"I'm telling you, something isn't right," he repeated.

"Ella?" I called out again moving towards the decorated staircase.

When my foot hit the first riser, the overhead lights in the lobby flickered and went out. I froze in place as the temperature dropped. The only light in the room was coming from the gentle gold and orange LED lights twinkling in the fall garland wrapped around the wooden banister.

Jacob stepped beside me. "What's happening?" His words made little puffs in the suddenly cold air.

"This is paranormal activity." While I waited for my eyes to adjust to the dimness, I slid the file folder on the bottom step. Pulling my cell phone from my back pocket, I switched it to video record. "Time 4:38 pm," I said, and added the date.

"What are you doing?" Jacob hissed at me.

"I'm investigating," I said, starting up the steps. "I used to do paranormal investigations when I was in grad school."

He gaped at me. "Like a ghost hunter?"

"Yes, I worked with a local team. I can sense spirits."

"Seriously?"

I rolled my eyes. "I don't have time to debate this," I whispered. "If you're afraid, wait here. But I'm going up."

CHAPTER SEVEN

As quietly as possible I started up the staircase. Jacob must have decided to tag along, either that or I'd pricked his male pride, because I could sense him walking right behind me.

"The nursery is on the third-floor," I said, breathing the words. "I want to see for myself what scared Donna so badly." Using a cell phone to try and record anything paranormal wasn't ideal, but it was all I had on hand. Aiming the camera on the phone outward, I went to the third floor.

Jacob tried a light switch at the top of the hall, but everything remained dark. "Why are all the lights off?" he asked softly.

It would take too long to explain it to him.

"Leave them," I said instead. Taking a firm grip on his wrist, I drew him with me.

"The crying stopped," he said.

I held a finger to my lips for silence.

He nodded in reply and gestured for me to go ahead. We traveled down the dark hall, and Jacob stayed right beside me as I moved to the open nursery door.

Standing in the doorway, I released his wrist and scanned the space. The room was empty of furniture and the windows were open. There was a drop cloth on the floor, and the paints Donna had used for the mural were out and open. I spotted a paintbrush a few feet away from the paint palette, where it had been dropped on the cloth.

"There's nothing here." His voice was hushed. "Nothing's moving except those old curtains in the breeze."

I slid my eyes to the open window and was starting to relax a bit...and then remembered that there were *no* curtains in the room.

With a gasp, I swung the phone back to the window. "Those aren't curtains in the breeze." I said.

"Jesus." Jacob recoiled.

The fact that he didn't bolt spoke well of him, because my heart had slammed hard in my chest. The semi-transparent shape by the window was vaguely female. I caught impressions of a long gown and dark hair. As we stood in the doorway staring, the distinct sound of crying filled the room once more.

Her sobs tore at my heart. "Bridgette?" I called.

The crying stopped and the apparition floated closer. Jacob snagged my arm, pulling me with him across to the opposite side of the hall. As we watched, her image faded. I could slightly make out an indistinct shape moving down the hallway past us, and toward the staircase.

Then it was gone.

"That was a *ghost*." Jacob's breath exploded out.

Sagging against the paneled hallway, I forced myself to exhale, giddy at seeing the apparition again. "It sure was."

Jacob's eyes were huge. "An actual ghost!"

"A collective apparition! That was amazing!" Caught up in the moment, I tossed my arms around his neck and gave him an enthusiastic hug.

His arms closed automatically around me. "Cammy," his voice was low.

I pulled back and searched his face. For a few long moments we stood in each other's arms. He didn't move a muscle the entire time. I wasn't sure if that was out of surprise at the experience, or because he was uncomfortable with my embrace.

"Sorry." I dropped my arms and stepped back. "I got over-excited with witnessing a collective apparition—that's a ghost seen by more than one person," I explained." Belatedly, I remembered to switch off the video recording on my phone.

"I...I just..." Jacob stopped and blew out a long breath. "Well, there's something you don't see everyday."

A helpless snort of laughter escaped me.

"What?" he scowled in my direction.

I couldn't stop the grin that spread over my face. "The last thing I ever expected out of you was to quote the *Ghostbusters*, in the face of a level two phenomena."

He leaned against the wall next to me. "Level two?"

"Seeing her, hearing her cry—any haunting that involves the physical senses," I said. "That's typically a level two phenomenon."

"You really do know about this supernatural stuff, don't you?"

"There are more things in heaven and earth, Horatio." I tossed the quote at him.

"Now you're quoting Hamlet."

"A landscaper who knows Shakespeare?" I raised an eyebrow. "What strange magick is this?"

"Smart-ass," Jacob chuckled. "I don't know why, but I kinda like that about you."

"Did you give me a compliment?"

"Yes." He stared at me intensely. "I did give you a compliment."

"Talk about your paranormal phenomenon..." I said, and watched his lips curve in reaction to my snark.

"All joking aside though," he said. "Jaime's been telling me for weeks that he's been seeing a lady in the windows of the mansion."

"He has?" My mind raced with possibilities.

Jacob nodded. "Yeah, he even waves to her. He's been telling me that he gave her some of his toys so she wouldn't be lonely."

"His toys?" I remembered the first day I met him. Jaime had said something about toys and had asked if I was 'the lady'.

"All this time I thought he been talking about Gabriella—or that he had an imaginary friend." Jacob suddenly looked uneasy. "Jaime even tried to point the lady out to me. I assumed that he had an overactive imagination. But now, I'm not sure."

"You didn't happen to see what section of the house he was waving at, did you?" I asked.

"The west side." His voice was thoughtful. "Third floor."

"Gabriella wouldn't be over there." I said, remembering that when my sister and Philippe had taken me over, that Gabriella had been wearing a dust mask.

"What's going on in this house?" Jacob demanded. "Is someone playing a prank on us?"

"No." I shook my head. "I truly don't think so."

"I honestly don't think so either." He glanced over at me. "You're not even afraid. Are you?"

"This isn't the first time I've seen the ghost," I said. "About eleven years ago, I saw a lady in white on the top floor of the western wing."

"You did?" he asked.

"I did." I nodded. "I was only fourteen at the time. That encounter is what got me interested in paranormal investigations."

"Cammy?" Gabriella's voice coming from the second-floor landing had us both flinching in surprise. "What's going on? Why are you standing up there in the dark?"

"We had a run in with your ghost," I called down to her. "Your resident spirit terrified the mural painter," I said.

"Shit!" Gabriella rushed up the stairs.

"She's gone now," I said.

"The ghost or Donna?" Gabriella asked.

I took my sister's arm to steady her as she hit the top of the steps. "Donna ran out of here crying a little while ago."

"Oh, no." Gabriella took a few steps down the hall, and on cue the lights flickered to life. She scowled at the overhead light fixture.

"Stupid circuit breaker. I hate it when the lights do that."

"I think the circuit breaker is the least of your problems, Sis," I said.

"Allow me my illusions," Gabriella said, peering down the hallway. "Is the ghost done for the time being, Cammy?"

"Probably," I said. "Paranormal activity tends to flare up, fade away and go dormant for a period of time."

"Why?" Jacob asked.

"The theory being that it takes the spirit a lot of energy to manifest," I explained. "Then it takes time for it to build that energy back up, in order to manage another appearance."

"I wonder where it goes to when it's finished for the day?" Gabriella asked, going to check the nursery.

"The ghost sort of melted through a wall." Jacob pointed down the hall. "Right over there."

"You saw her too?" Gabriella asked Jacob.

"I saw something," he said. "I'm having trouble wrapping my mind around it at the moment."

I splayed my fingers wide on either side of my head, making an explosion sound. "The skeptic's mind has been officially blown."

Gabriella placed a hand on Jacob's arm. "I'm sorry for all of this."

He smiled at my sister. "There's no need to apologize."

"Why don't we go down to the kitchen?" Gabriella suggested. "You two deserve a drink after your close encounter—"

"That's the term for UFOs, Ella," I said. "Not hauntings."

"Whatever," Gabriella said. "You can fill me in on what you both experienced."

The three of us trooped down the stairs. Jacob kindly picked up the grocery bags from where my sister had dropped them on the landing. I went and retrieved my research file and took it to the kitchen. He set the bags on the counter, and at my sister's insistence, he took a seat at the kitchen island. Shadow came wandering in and hopped up on the counter to stare at the visitor.

While Gabriella put her groceries away, I went to the fridge, got us both a beer, and handed my sister a bottle of apple juice. Removing the tops off all the bottles, I passed them around, tapping my beer to Jacob's. "Here's to not freaking out on me, Venkmen."

He laughed. "Pleasure working with you, Dr. Spengler."

The *Ghostbusters* reference had Gabriella chuckling. Philippe strolled in, saw us all, and stopped.

"You might want to sit down, babe," Gabriella said. She smirked at his blank expression and got out another beer.

"What has happened?" he asked.

"Donna apparently ran crying from the house today." Gabriella handed him the beer. "And Camilla and Jacob got an up-close and personal with our ghost shortly thereafter."

"Is Donna alright?" Philippe asked.

"She was pretty scared," I said. "When she ran out, Jacob and I went in to check on Gabriella."

"I dash off to the market for fifteen minutes, and all hell breaks loose," Gabriella groused, folding up her shopping bags. "That'll teach me."

"Camilla, tell me what happened." Philippe sat beside Jacob at the kitchen island. "I am, as you say, all ears."

I took the remaining bar stool and started from when I'd parked the car and spoken to Jacob. The video on my phone *had* picked up a blur of movement and the faintest of crying. "It's hardly conclusive proof," I said. "However, it is something interesting you can have to back up your two eye-witnesses accounts."

"Incredible." Philippe whistled. "I've lived here for a year and have heard the occasional crying. I've dealt with the cold spots and the flickering lights...but other than that, nothing."

"I saw her in the window, once," Gabriella admitted. "And I've heard her crying since I moved in. I've been keeping a journal of every time something ghostly goes on."

"I'd like to see that journal," I said.

"Sure," Gabriella said. "I've been leaving it in the tower room."

"Did you talk to Jaime about any of these experiences?" Jacob asked her.

"No." Gabriella's voice was firm. "Of course

not."

"He's been seeing her too," Jacob said, with a sigh. Then he shared with Philippe and Gabriella what his little boy had told him about the lady he'd seen in the windows of the western wing.

"Could this all be because I'm living here now?" Gabriella wondered. "Is she upset about the baby? You both—and apparently Donna—saw her in the nursery."

"Jaime is interacting with her—giving her his toys," I thought out loud. "Now she's appearing in the nursery. I'm inclined to think Bridgette likes children. Jaime isn't afraid of her, and that says it all." I took another sip of my beer.

"Wait. Why do you call it—her, Bridgette?" Jacob asked.

"That's my working theory," I said. "I think the ghost haunting the Marquette Mansion is the spirit of Bridgette Ames."

"Ames?" Jacob's eyebrows went up. "Her last name was *Ames*? Are you freaking kidding me?"

"No, I'm not kidding you," I said, surprised

at his reaction. "Bridgette Ames was the bride of Pierre Michel Marquette, but she disappeared in 1847. Some folks think she may have been murdered by her husband, others wonder if she ran off."

"They never found her body," Philippe said solemnly. "To my knowledge no one in my family knows what happened to her."

"I was able to find some new information today," I said, pushing the folder closer to Philippe. Getting out my phone again, I showed them the photos I'd taken of the Ames family display from the genealogical museum. "I already emailed the pictures I took to both you and Gabriella," I told Philippe.

"So that's what she looked like." Gabriella's voice was thoughtful as she studied the image of Bridgette.

Jacob considered the image on the phone, and then his eyes shifted to my face. "You're absolutely sure," he said. "That the bride's maiden name was Ames?"

"Yes," Philippe answered before I could. "We have the documentation, copies of the marriage license."

Jacob set his beer down with shaking hands. "Well, holy shit."

I frowned. "After everything else, why does *that* freak you out?"

"You don't know?" he asked.

"Know what?"

"Cammy," he said. "My last name is Ames."

A loud bang from somewhere above us punctuated his words.

Jacob flinched at the noise. Gabriella scowled at the ceiling. Shadow yawned, Philippe shook his head, and I considered the modern-day Ames sitting next to me.

This was an eerie coincidence, I thought, *Even for a daughter of Midnight.*

I cleared my throat. "Jacob, do you live in the long stone house in the village? The two story with the red shutters and gingerbread on the front porch?" I reached out and flipped open the file of research that I'd gathered from the genealogical library. I thumbed through the papers searching for the photocopy of the drawing of the Ames family house.

"Why do you ask?" Jacob said, suspiciously.

"Is this your house?" I handed him the copy

of the drawing of the unique stone building.

"Yes." He nodded. "That's my family's home."

I felt a slight tingle as everything started to fall together. "Which means you're descended from Jonah Ames Sr., the man who owned the stone quarry."

"That's right." Jacob nodded.

"His son, Jonah Ames Jr. was the older brother of Bridgette," I said. "Which makes Bridgette Ames, an ancestor of yours."

"Good god," Philippe breathed.

I placed my hand on Jacob's arm. "I think, we have our answer as to why the manifestations are suddenly ramping up."

***

I stood on the pretty brick landing of the side entrance to the mansion with the Halloween lights at my back, watching Jacob drive his truck down the service road and out past the winery shop.

Even after the revealing talk with Gabriella and Philippe, Jacob still had to get home to his son. I'd walked him back down to the lobby and the ceiling lights were burning as if nothing unusual had ever happened.

"Well," he'd said. "See you around." He handed over the invoice and I promised to pass it on to Philippe.

"Good night." I had walked him to the door. He seemed troubled, almost like he needed a hug, but instead, I settled for sending him a reassuring smile.

I'd have to talk to him again, I thought as I watched Jacob drive away. I had absolutely no idea how he would react to seeing me, considering all that had happened. But I would have to try. I needed to interview the Ames family as well. Jaime too, if he was comfortable with that. At least now we knew why Bridgette was becoming more active. Her descendants were in and around the mansion.

I thought back to the time I'd first seen the ghost. She'd told me that *the prophecy awaits...* I still had no idea what that actually meant, but maybe the Ames family would know.

***

A few days later had me returning to my booth at the garden center. The pumpkin spice lip balm was selling as fast as I could make it, and I brought an even bigger batch with me this time. I filled up the first lip balm holder and arranged a secondary display. The melt and pour celestial shaped soaps were all gone, and I pulled out my phone to make a quick reminder note to make more.

I tidied up the display table and was heading towards the back exit when I spotted Max and Jacob in the office. I figured they were having a meeting about a landscaping project, and my intention had been to give Max a casual wave on my way out, but that changed when I heard their conversation.

"Listen, Max. I'm asking you if Jaime is safe being around the Midnight family."

Jacob's back was to me and since neither man had seen me, I ducked back out of sight, eavesdropping shamelessly from around the corner.

"Jacob." Max's voice was no-nonsense. "Don't be ridiculous. I have known the

Midnights for a long time. Gabriella and I have been friends, close friends, for years. Nicole and I were married in their gardens last month. They're good people, and are like family to me."

"What about the Marquette mansion? Is it safe?" Jacob's anxious voice carried clearly out to the sales floor. "I've got people I barely know telling me that my ancestor was probably murdered up in that spooky old house two hundred years ago, and I had no idea of any of this when I allowed Jaime to hang out with Gabriella *inside* that place a few weeks ago."

"I thought they baked cookies together," Max said calmly.

"They did."

"Did Jaime enjoy himself?"

"He had a blast," Jacob replied.

"So what's your problem?" Max asked.

"There's some crazy shit going on up there!" Jacob's voice went up. "If I hadn't seen it with my own eyes I'd never believe it. Gabriella is terrific, and Philippe Marquette seems like a nice enough man, but there's a god-damn ghost roaming the halls of his house! I'm still having a hard time with accepting it."

"I can't speak to the ghostly stuff," Max said. "But I *can* tell you that neither Gabriella or Philippe would ever do anything to harm or to frighten your son."

"What can you tell me about Cammy?" Jacob's tone of voice changed.

"What about her?" Max asked. "Are you interested in her?"

Yes, what about me? I crossed my arms and continued to listen.

"Well she's gorgeous, but I'm having trouble getting past..." Jacob paused. "She's really into the occult, isn't she?"

"Maybe you should ask her about that," said Max.

My face flushed red, listening to their conversation. I took a quick peek around the corner, far enough to see Max and Jacob sitting across the desk from each other. Max appeared calm, and while there was no anger coming from Jacob, I did sense confusion, and some worry.

"I did ask her about it. She didn't deny a thing." Jacob said with a sigh. "But at first, I thought she was joking and I teased her about it a bit. That seemed to piss her off. Which pretty much ruined any chance I might have had to ask her out."

Max shrugged. "If she's into magick, why would that be an issue for you?"

"I'm a father," Jacob said. "I would never knowingly expose my son to anything dangerous. But he's begging to see her again, and wants go to her house for Halloween. Would that be wise, considering?"

Oh for goddess sake! I rolled my eyes. *What did he expect, that I lived in a gingerbread house and was plotting to lure Jaime inside?*

Max threw back his head and laughed. "Listen to yourself, man."

"Clearly, I've lost my damn mind." Jacob hunched his shoulders a bit. "I'm seriously out of practice. Maybe it's because I haven't been interested in a woman for a long time. Not after Jaime's mother...and even you have to admit that Camilla Midnight *is* different."

"Let me ask you this," Max said. "How was Jaime around Cammy? Did your boy seem afraid or act nervous around her?"

"No he didn't," Jacob answered. "He can't stop talking about her. He's drawn a dozen pictures of a lady with pink hair holding a basket full of soap."

Max chuckled.

Awww, I thought. *What a sweet little boy.*

"It's that pink hair of hers that hooked me," Jacob said. "I'm into a woman who has a pierced nose, green eyes, pink hair, and who is in all probability—a Witch."

"Cammy is one of a kind," Max said, sounding like a proud older brother.

"Even my mother likes her," Jacob said with a sigh. "Mom would smack me upside the head if she knew how I'd spoken to Cammy the other day."

"Jenna *would* kick your ass," Max said, and Jacob laughed in reluctant agreement.

I had to cover my mouth so as not to laugh out loud. *I knew I liked that woman.* I'd heard more than enough, and began to ease back.

"Seems to me..." Max's voice still carried clearly across the room. "You have some apologizing to do."

I stepped away, silently moving further from

the office. I deliberately retreated to the booth space, picked up a lip balm, counted to ten, and then walked—loudly—toward the office area again. When I reached the doorway, I stopped.

"Oh, hi Max!" I said brightly, as though surprised. "I didn't know you were here."

Jacob shot to his feet and stood staring at me. It was very, very, gratifying to see a faint blush of red creep up his neck. "Camilla," he stammered slightly.

I handed Jacob the lip balm. "I believe you were wanting one of these the other day."

"Oh, yeah. Thanks," he said. "Thank you. That was very kind of you."

I met his eyes, and held them for a few moments. "Don't mention it."

Max sat in his chair, grinning. "Nicole says we've been selling your items pretty steadily since the Harvest Festival. At this rate, you're going to outgrow us and need to open your own shop sooner than later."

"We'll see," I said to Max. Purposefully fluffing the ends of my hair, I watched Jacob's eyes follow the movement. "How's that shaving soap working for you?" I asked him.

"The what?" Jacob stared blankly.

"The shaving soap you bought the other day." I reminded him gently.

"Oh, yeah." He cleared his throat. "The soap. It works great."

Casually, I checked my watch, "Well I better head home, I have some jack-o'-lanterns to carve for tomorrow night's trick-or-treaters." I waited a beat and smiled at Jacob. "I hope you and Jaime can drop by. I have some nut-free treats especially for him."

"Sure," he said. "Jaime would like that."

"Well, then we'll see you tomorrow evening." I stepped out of the office. "Catch you later, Max." I blew a kiss towards Max and sashayed straight out the back door. I resisted the urge to do a fist pump, telling myself not to be too arrogant.

CHAPTER EIGHT

The holiday of Samhain, the old Celtic new year, officially began at sunset on October thirty-first. What was once an ancient festival celebrating the end of the agricultural year, and the final harvest of the autumn, had morphed into today's All Hallows Eve—or Halloween.

This year, we'd been blessed with warm temperatures. It was warm enough that I'd worn a Halloween t-shirt, jeans, and was currently barefoot. A lopsided gibbous moon shone down, and there was enough of a breeze to send fallen leaves scuttling across the grass. Now that the sun had set, I had tucked the last of the candles inside of the jack-o'-lanterns and lit them one by one.

I went down the front steps, out to the lawn,

and studied the overall effect. The bundles of cornstalks we'd attached to the main porch posts rustled spookily in the breeze, and the baskets of brown and orange mums were showing off their spicy blooms. I was glad I'd gone ahead and added a few rustic lanterns with LED candles at various points on the steps and around the flowers and pumpkins. The orange lights strung along the porch lit up the front of the farmhouse with a cheerful glow. It was warm, inviting, and charming.

With a contented sigh, I wiggled my bare toes and tipped my head back to study the sky. The veil between the world of the living and the spirit was at its thinnest tonight, and I wondered how Gabriella and Philippe were doing up at the mansion. I blew a kiss to the waxing moon, taking a moment to remember my father Daniel, and my grandfather, who had both passed on.

Halloween, had always been one of my favorite days of the year. For wise women and cunning men, this was a sacred night. One where the ancestors were honored and the community gathered together. As was tradition,

I'd set up an ancestor altar on a table in the living room. I'd displayed photos of my father and grandfather, and Gran had added photos of her parents as well.

"I brought the candy out." My grandmother's voice carried to me from the front porch.

I saw that Gran was holding a large cast-iron cauldron. I hustled up the steps to take it from her. "Let me help you." Together we placed the candy-filled cauldron on a table.

"You've done a lovely job with the decorations this year, Camilla," Gran said.

I tucked my tongue in my cheek. "I wish I could go all out with tombstones, and bats, a vampire coffin, maybe even one of those funny Witches who looks like it crashed into a tree."

"Not while I still have breath in my body," Gran said—as I knew she would.

I couldn't help the laugh that bubbled up. "Gotcha."

Gran shook her head. "Why you insist upon yanking my chain, I'll never know."

I pressed a kiss to her cheek. "Because it's fun."

"This past year has brought many changes to

our family," Gran said, slipping her arm in mine.

"Um, hm." I agreed. "By the time the wheel of the year makes another full turn, Gabriella and Dru will both be married and the baby will be here."

"I don't mind saying the thought of two weddings *and* a baby in the next year makes me feel a little overwhelmed," Gran said.

"It's going to be busy *and* exciting."

"And how about you, young lady?" Gran said. "How's your love life?"

I shrugged. "Nonexistent."

"That's not what I hear," Gran said breezily.

I gawked at her. "What are you talking about?"

"Jacob Ames," she said casually. "How is your handsome young man from the garden center?"

My jaw dropped. I had no idea how she'd gotten wind of that. "He's not *my* young man," I said, firmly.

She patted my shoulder. "He's certainly more close-minded than your usual type of beau, sweetheart."

"Oh my goddess. Gran, I..." Shutting my eyes, I took a steadying breath and tried again. "No one says *beau*, anymore Gran."

"Alright." Gran nodded. "Then he's not your usual type of lover—"

"Jacob Ames is *not* my lover!" I cut her off.

"Not yet," Gran predicted.

"What do you know?" I demanded. "What have you seen?"

She reached up and cupped my face in her hands. "There are some things even a wise woman can't fight, my girl."

I studied her wise blue eyes. "Meaning what?"

"There is a prophecy."

"*What*?" I demanded.

She hushed me. "All will be revealed in good time. For now, trust in the knowledge that you will fulfill this destiny in your own unique way." When I would have argued, she pressed a kiss to my forehead. "Patience," she said. "Let's enjoy the evening, and give out candy to the trick-or-treaters."

I was about to insist for more information, but headlights flashed in the driveway. A van full of children began to pile out. I wasn't sure what to make of my grandmother's odd prediction. However, when a second group of children came trooping up the driveway, I shifted over fully to candy duty and decided to enjoy myself.

We'd been handing out treats to the kids for about an hour when a familiar truck pulled into our driveway. Jacob stepped from his truck and swung Jaime down to the driveway. The boy took one look at the farmhouse and was racing up the front sidewalk, waving.

"Hi Cammy!" Jaime skidded to a halt at the base of the steps. "Trick or treat!"

"It's the Flash!" I feigned shock. "Gran! It's a superhero!"

Gran stepped beside me. "Well as I live and breathe..." she said breathlessly.

"It's me, Cammy," he laughed. "It's Jaime!"

I narrowed my eyes at him. "You shot up the sidewalk so fast I thought it was the real Flash." I reached into the cauldron holding the candy and pulled out a couple of nut-free chocolate bars and a homemade popcorn ball.

Jacob caught up to his son. "Happy

Halloween," he said formally.

"Happy Halloween," I said, dropping the candy in Jaime's plastic pumpkin. "No peanuts."

"Thanks." Jacob nodded. "We have to be extra careful tonight."

"I can't eat any candy 'til my Grandma and Grandpa check it all," Jaime said, soberly.

"That's smart." I patted the top of his head. "We don't want you to get sick."

"Your pumpkins look great," Jacob said, admiring the jack-o'-lanterns.

"Thank you." Gran inclined her head. "As wise women, we enjoy celebrating the seasons and the old festival days."

I squinted over at my grandmother. Her statement had been smooth, but the gravity of the statement had dropped into the casual conversation like a ton of bricks.

"Yes, ma'am." Jacob nodded to her respectfully. "I understand."

"Do you?" she asked him with a cool smile.

"Dad," Jaime piped up before his father could reply. "My pumpkin is almost full. I won't be able to fit anymore candy in here."

"When I was little," I told the boy, "my sisters and I used pillowcases for trick-or-treating."

Jaime pushed his mask further back. "I could put a lot more candy in that..."

"Would you like to borrow one?" Gran asked, which is how we ended up inviting the Ames boys inside.

Gran went and fetched a pillowcase for Jaime. He happily followed her, telling how Gabriella and Philippe had given him homemade sugar cookies. Which left me standing awkwardly in the living room with his father.

"Nice shirt," Jacob said as soon as we were alone.

Automatically, I glanced down. My shirt was gray with the words: *Resting Witch Face* written across the front. "I thought it was amusing."

He chuckled at that. "I'm almost disappointed that you're not dressed in flowing black."

I raised one eyebrow. "I'd hate to be accused of being a cliché."

Jacob's gaze took in the living room. I tried to see it through his eyes. The comfy leather sofa, brick fireplace, the decorated mantle filled with orange pumpkins, colorful leaves, black silk roses, and twinkling autumn lights. I could literally watch his shoulders drop as he began to relax.

"This is a great house," he said.

"Thank you." I inclined my head. "Were you expecting an *Addams Family* mansion style of interior? Perhaps with a coffin for a coffee table?"

"Of course not," he said defensively.

I crossed my arms over my chest and tipped my head to one side. "I suppose I should be flattered that you don't consider anything here too *dangerous* for Jaime."

His mouth dropped open. "You overheard me yesterday." It was a statement. Not a question.

Before I could answer, I saw through the living room window a group of youngsters running up the sidewalk toward the house. "Excuse me for a minute." I quickly moved outside to the porch and greeted the kids. I passed out candy to a few young zombies and a princess, complimenting their costumes.

"Thank you. Happy Halloween!" the children cried, and they were off and down the steps.

"Happy Halloween!" I waved to the children's parents who waited at the end of the driveway.

Jacob followed me out to the porch. "I'm sorry," he said as soon as the children were out of earshot.

I considered him from over my shoulder. "Are you?"

Cautiously, he rested a hand on my arm. "I am sorry if I offended you. Honestly, I've never met anyone like you before, Camilla. I'm sort of learning as I go."

He was earnest in his apology, which softened me the tiniest bit. However, the attraction I felt for him annoyed me. That annoyance, I assured myself, was the only reason I had to concentrate to keep up with the conversation. *Goddess, he looked mighty fine in that chambray work shirt...*I thought, and then my brain caught up with my hormones. *Hang on. What had he just said?* Mentally, I backtracked. "Anyone like me?" I repeated.

"What do you mean by that exactly, Jacob?"

His eyes met mine. "This magick thing you and your family are into...it's a sort of spiritual path, right?"

I took a careful breath and fought to stay composed. "That's one way of saying it."

Jacob nodded in acknowledgement of my words. He slid his hand down to my wrist, and he turned it over and studied the small triple moon tattoo there. "This is pretty," he said. "I noticed it the other day at the garden center but didn't get a chance to ask you about it. What does it mean?"

"It's a triple goddess symbol," I said.

"Triple goddess?"

I studied him closely. He was listening, and I detected no skepticism, only curiosity. "The triple goddess," I said, "represents the three faces of the goddess, and three main points in a woman's life. The Maiden, Mother and Crone. These aspects are symbolized by the waxing crescent, the full moon and the waning crescent."

"What aspect are you currently?" His voice was polite. In fact he was so respectful that it took me a moment before I answered him.

"The Maiden," I said.

"Maiden?" He frowned. "That doesn't mean that you're a—"

"Virgin?" I finished for him. "No. The term 'Maiden' means whole, as in I belong to no-one and am *whole unto myself.*" I held my breath waiting for a snide comment, but there was none.

He nodded, thinking that over. "Gabriella would be like the Mother aspect of the goddess..."

I was surprised at how quickly he caught on. "That's correct."

"Okay I get it." he smiled. "Her baby belly is shaped like the full moon." He made a curved motion with his hands. "As in round."

"Exactly." I nodded.

"And your grandmother would be an aspect of—"

"The Crone," I said.

"Like the classic, old wise woman..." Jacob smiled. "I can totally see that."

I blinked. "I must say, this is a big shift of attitude from only a few days ago."

"I've been doing a little research," he said, running his thumb over my tattoo.

My pulse jumped as his thumb stroked over the symbols on my inner wrist. "Please tell me you didn't get all of your information off some silly site on the internet."

"No." He stepped closer. "I went to the library."

"That must have been a refreshing change of pace for you," I said tartly.

"I probably deserved that." He chuckled. "You know this is most likely the longest conversation we've had—that didn't end with you being angry at me."

"The night is young," I predicted.

"Then I guess there's no harm in doing this." He stepped in and slid his arms around my waist.

Even as he leaned closer, I pulled back. "What do you think you're doing?" I asked.

Jacob smiled. "I'm attracted to you," he said. "I know that you know that. So let's not play any more games."

"I'm not playing," I argued. "I simply think you're getting *way* ahead of yourself."

"We'll see. Shut up and kiss me, Camilla." And with that, he pressed his lips firmly to mine.

I don't know what I'd expected. Maybe a pleasant tingle or perhaps a nice jolt of attraction...but the heart slamming, stomach flipping, *oh-my-goddess* hormonal explosion was *not* it.

Stunned at the intensity, I stood there and let him kiss me. He ended the kiss with the smallest of nips to my bottom lip, and I had to suppress a moan of pleasure. Simultaneously, we broke apart, and stared at each other. The moment stretched long between us, and all I could hear was my own pulse thundering in my ears.

Let's try that again, I thought, and reaching up, I grabbed a hold of his shirt collar and yanked him back down to me. I wrapped my hands around his head and held him firmly in place as we kissed. This time, our mouths were fully open and our tongues began to duel. Dimly, I recognized that his hands were roaming down my back and molding over my butt.

When he tugged me closer our hips collided, and I could feel how much he wanted me. I think it was that more than anything else that had us both stopping. We pulled apart—far enough to see each other's faces, and stood there breathing heavily.

"I really want you." Jacob's voice was a deep growl of sound. "I'm not going to try and hide that."

"I know," I said. "To my surprise, the feeling is mutual."

"What do you suggest we do about that?"

I crossed my arms over my chest. I knew it was a defensive posture, but I didn't care. "We could wait and see if it passes," I suggested.

Jaime's bright laughter drifted out to us. He was still chattering to Gran. Jacob glanced back to the front door. "I should go back inside and check on Jaime."

I stood there and waited, wondering what he would do next. For a second I thought Jacob was going to kiss me again, it was in his eyes, but a familiar SUV pulled into our driveway, and I saw that my sister and Brooke had arrived.

The spell broken, we stepped apart.

"Happy Halloween!" Dru called as she and Brooke started up the sidewalk.

"Nice costumes," I said, telling myself to smile. Drusilla was wearing all blue and had on a long tulle skirt with matching faerie wings. Brooke skipped up the steps and was wearing a black shirt, short lime green tulle skirt, striped tights and neon green fairy wings.

"We decided to dress up like the faeries from Dru's books," Brooke said, straightening the floral crown she wore. "Dru made me a costume like the character in her newest story —the one that she named after me."

"You are a dead ringer for your faerie namesake," I gave the girl a hug.

"That's because Dru had her artist work from my picture!" Brooke announced excitedly.

"So you're famous now." I rolled my eyes. "They'll be no living with her after this," I said to my sister.

Dru pressed a finger to her cheek as if thinking it over. "Let's hope, for all our sakes, that the notoriety doesn't go to her head."

Brooke began to laugh. "Where's Gran? I

wanna show her my costume." The girl spun around and rushed in the house, calling for our grandmother.

Dru slanted a considering look at me, and then over toward Jacob. "Hello, Jacob, it's nice to see you." Her voice was perfectly polite and put me on guard.

"Hello." He nodded at Dru. "I heard you and Garrett got engaged. Congratulations."

"Thank you." Drusilla smiled and then excused herself. She walked to the door and wiggled her eyebrows at me from behind Jacob's back.

I bit my lip trying to keep a straight face. Dru grinned, gave me a thumbs up, and followed Brooke inside. Alone again with Jacob I wasn't sure exactly what to say. I almost jumped when Jacob began speaking.

"Meet me for coffee at the Café in Grafton tomorrow morning?" he asked.

"I don't drink coffee."

"They serve tea there," Jacob said quietly. "I want to see you, Camilla. To get to know you better."

He was unexpectedly smooth, I thought. *You*

had to give him points for that. "What time?" I asked.

"It will have to be early," Jacob said.

"I can handle early."

He reached out and took my hand. "Seven o'clock."

I gave his fingers a small squeeze. "Okay, I'll meet you at seven."

He gave my hand the briefest of squeezes back. Then he let go, pulled open the screen door for me, and we walked back in the farmhouse.

***

We met for coffee the next morning and spent a pleasant half hour together. By unspoken agreement, we kept the conversation limited to his landscaping work, gardening, my soap making, and Jaime's night of trick-or-treating. It amazed me how charming he could be when he wasn't being a cynic.

Over the next few weeks, we began dating. We kept it casual for the most part, meeting for coffee, or hiking at a local park. We went out for beer and burgers at a dive in Alton. We even took Jaime to the movies and finished up with dinner at a pizza place. At my invitation, Jacob brought Jaime over to the farmhouse on a weeknight, and I made them spaghetti. Gran enjoyed the company, and Jaime had gotten a huge kick out of seeing all my soap-making supplies.

Gran chatted with Jacob about putting in a water feature in the gardens next spring, and after supper Jaime ran around the back gardens of the farmhouse while we all sat around the fire pit. We'd made S'mores and enjoyed a cozy evening.

We never spoke again about magick—and that was tricky for me. It was so much a part of my identity that I had to be very careful when I talked to Jacob, and having to hold most of myself back made me decide to take the dating *very* slowly.

The last thing I'd ever expected was to end up in an old-fashioned romance with a single father, but all things considered, being cautious was my wisest course of action. I'd never taken this much time getting to know someone before. There was plenty of heat between the two of us, but I wasn't in a rush to head straight to the bedroom. Besides, I wanted to see if he was humoring me, or if anything he'd said to me on Halloween night was sincere.

November rolled on, and I'd begun to search for a place in the village to open my own shop. I had contacted a realtor and began negotiations for the lease on a building that had once housed a boutique. It was in a good location, two blocks uphill from the Great River Road, and in the middle of our small historic district. The building was two doors down from the general store, and across the street from the information center where the tourists went to learn more about the history of the village.

When Jacob invited me over to his house for dinner the Sunday before Thanksgiving, I wasn't sure if his folks would be home, or if it would be only the two of us alone. I dressed carefully in a slouchy, off the shoulder, moss green sweater that played up my eyes. I paired the top with black jeans, added a pair of dangling silver and peridot earrings, and zipped up my knee length boots over the jeans. I brought along a bottle of white wine from the *Trois Amis* winery and tossed on a black jacket.

The drive to the village proper was a short one. I pulled up in front of the long stone house his family lived in and parked my car at the curb. Like many of the houses in Ames Crossing, there was no front yard to speak of, however the historic home was inviting with big wooden rocking chairs on the deep covered porch and the bright red shutters that popped against the limestone.

Someone had begun decorating for the holidays. All the window boxes on the lower level were filled with evergreen boughs. I took a deep breath, squared my shoulders and knocked on the front door.

An older man answered the door. His resemblance to Jacob was strong enough that I knew immediately it was his father. "Hello." He smiled. "You must be Camilla."

I stuck my hand out. "You must be Jacob's father."

He brushed my hand aside and gave me a welcoming hug. "We don't stand on ceremony around here, girl."

I patted his back in response to the friendly bear hug and was tugged inside. I had a few seconds to sum up the house. Wide old plank floors, sturdy furniture, and colorful rugs. A fire crackled in a stone hearth, and a massive television was set up across the room, where a football game blared.

"Jeremiah," sounded a woman's voice. "I told you to turn down the TV *before* she got here." The sound of the game was muted as Jacob's mother aimed, clicked, and tossed the remote on the seat of a wide leather recliner.

"Hello, Mrs. Ames," I said holding out the bottle of wine. "Thank you for inviting me to your home."

"Jenna," she corrected me. "You can call me Jenna." She accepted the bottle of wine, looped her arm in mine and hauled me off to a large sunny kitchen. "Jacob will be right down," she said.

"Oh wow," I said, admiring the space. The walls were thick, gorgeous stone. The cabinets were a bright pop of white and were warmed up by practical butcher block countertops. The appliances were stainless steel, and colorful dishes gleamed from behind a few strategically placed glass-fronted cabinets. I tipped my head back, admiring the rustic beams in the ceiling. "What a gorgeous kitchen."

"The woman nagged me for years, until I re-did it all for her," Jeremiah said.

"After thirty-five years, we deserved an updated kitchen," Jenna said back.

"It did turn out nice, if I do say so myself." Jeremiah tucked his hands in his pockets.

"This kitchen is my pride and joy," she said. "Next to my children and grandchildren."

I ran my fingers over the long island where sturdy barstools invited guests to sit. "I can see why."

Jenna went to open the wine. She poured us each a glass and the three of us chatted easily. I heard a clatter, and Jaime came scrambling down the kitchen steps. Jacob followed at a more sedate pace.

Jaime launched himself at me, and I found myself with a lap full of five-year-old.

"You're here!" Jaime snuggled right in.

I pressed a kiss to the top of his head. "I had to spend some time with my favorite guy, didn't

I?"

"What about me?" Jacob walked directly to me and kissed me on the mouth—right in front of his parents.

CHAPTER NINE

It took everything I had *not* to be flustered.

Jeremiah chuckled. "She's turning the same color as her hair, son."

Jacob raised his eyebrows. "Camilla can handle herself."

With an effort I pulled myself together and gave Jenna a hand putting dinner on the table. While we ate a truly spectacular spinach lasagna, Jacob explained to me that he'd filled his parents in on the history of the Marquette mansion. Without using the words, *ghost* or *haunting*, we discussed it around the table. Jacob's parents were fascinated by the missing bride and her dowry that had disappeared. To my relief, the majority of the conversation went right over Jaime's head.

"My grandfather used to talk about the scandal from 1847," Jeremiah said. "I grew up hearing about Bridgette and how she vanished. My grandfather always insisted that the amethysts had been stolen, and that there'd been foul play."

"What's foul play?" Jaime wanted to know.

"It's when a chicken dances," his grandfather said smoothly, and Jaime thought that was hilarious.

"I did some digging through Jeremiah's family papers," Jenna said. "There's several boxes full of things up in the attic, including a journal I think you'd find interesting."

"I'd love to see it," I said. "I've been trying to research Philippe's family, but I've found more on the Ames clan, than the Marquette's."

After dinner was cleared, Jeremiah took Jaime outside to run him around the back yard. Jacob and I sat together at the kitchen island while his mother brought in a small box filled with papers. She lifted up an old leather-bound journal. "I discovered this quite by accident." Jenna passed the book to me. "It's the journal of Mary Ames and it goes from the years of 1845 to 1847."

"Mary was Bridgette's older sister." I took the journal gently and set it carefully on the countertop.

"That's right." Jenna nodded. "I flagged a few entries with sticky notes. Especially the ones where she writes about trying to go see her sister after her marriage to Pierre Michel, and that she was barred from the home, by the groom."

I blinked. "She was?"

"I think you should both see these entries," Jenna said soberly. "Mary wrote in her journal that she feared for her sister's safety."

"Oh no," I said, and flipped to the pages to read them for myself.

"Mom." Jacob frowned as we read. "I didn't know any of this."

"Well, neither did I." She shrugged. "But when you told your father and I about the goings on up at the mansion—and how Cammy thought it might be Bridgette Ames haunting the place..." Jenna stopped and cleared her throat. "We both decided it might be a good time to go through the family papers. When I found the journal—I read all of it. Then, I discussed it with your father."

"Okay." Jacob nodded.

The atmosphere in the room had gone from cheerful to intense almost instantly. I read for myself what Mary had written, and Jenna had quoted her almost word for word.

"For Mary, the missing jewels meant nothing," Jenna said gently. "She only wanted to know what had happened to her sister."

I nodded to Jenna. "It was Jonah Jr., wasn't it, who pushed to have the amethyst parure returned to the Ames family?"

"There's more you need to see." Jenna said. Flipping to a final hot pink sticky note. "This journal entry involves the Midnight family."

"*My* family?" I asked.

"Yes." Jenna adjusted her glasses. "After Bridgette had been missing for a few months, Mary went to see one of the Midnights in the village. A young woman named Victoria who was rumored to have had 'The Sight'."

I knew my family tree, and my heart sank, wondering how Jacob would respond to this information. "My grandfather did have a great-

great aunt named Victoria," I said.

"That must have been her," Jenna said.

"Sounds like it." I managed a polite nod in response, but I was casting my memories back to what I knew of the woman. *Victoria never married,* I recalled. *But was thought to have been the most gifted Seer of all the daughters of Midnight.*

"Victoria Midnight insisted that Bridgette was beyond this world," Jenna continued, pointing to those same words in the journal. "But, she did tell Mary that everything would be put to rights again when the prophecy was fulfilled."

My stomach flipped over at the words. "Prophecy?" I said, risking a look at Jacob to see how he was taking all the news.

"See for yourselves," Jenna nudged the book closer. "Mary wrote it all down."

I took the book in my hands and read the prophecy.

The house on the cliffs will be torn asunder,
One soul is damned and the other shall wander.
For the jewels to be recovered and the truth

to come to light,
Requires two sons of the Ames clan, and a
daughter of Midnight.
One son will show kindness, the other learns
to believe in what he sees,
While the daughter with roses for hair, must
accept her own destiny.
For she who mixes potions and balms, and
he who whispers to trees,
Together may find true love, restore peace,
and gain prosperity.

"Whoa," I breathed, and thought back to when I'd been only fourteen and had seen the ghost in the mansion for the first time...

The prophecy awaits, she'd said.

Silently, Jacob took the book from my hands. After finishing the entry, he gently set the journal down. The silence stretched in the kitchen for a good thirty seconds. "*Two* sons of the Ames clan?" he finally said.

"I'm betting that means you and Jaime." My voice shook.

Jacob nodded. "Which means the daughter of Midnight would be you."

Jenna rested a hand on my shoulder. "Roses

for hair," she pointed out, "would be the best way to describe pink dyed hair to a woman of the 1840's."

I nodded. "And then there's the whole, 'she who mixes potions and balms'."

"I suppose you would say, I whisper to trees," Jacob finished.

I glanced warily at him. He was taking it pretty well, all things considered, and then...

"This is insane!" Jacob shoved away from the counter. "Is this some sort of joke?"

I sighed, watching Jacob while he stalked across the kitchen floor. *Surprise, surprise,* I thought. *The skeptic was angry.*

"Before you accuse me of staging this," Jenna said to her son, "I'll invite you to closely inspect the pages of the journal. Check the texture of the paper and the fading of the ink. As you can see it's all consistent in the entire journal. This is very old. That prophecy wasn't recently added."

"Mom." Jacob stopped his pacing. "I know you'd never do something like that."

"Did you have any idea about all of this, Camilla?" Jenna wanted to know.

I dragged a hand through my hair. "My Gran warned me last month that there was a prophecy in play, but I'd forgotten about it, until now." I didn't dare mention what the ghost had said all those years ago...Jacob would flip. I sat very still for a moment and tried to process everything. "Would you mind if I took a few photographs of this journal, Jenna?"

She patted my shoulder. "You go right ahead."

I fetched the phone from my purse and took photos of the most pertinent pages. "Philippe will want to see these," I said. *Plus, I wanted to show the prophecy to Gran. Had she been aware of all the details?* I wondered. *Or had her intuition simply clued her in?*

Jenna volunteered to put Jaime to bed, and I left a short time later. I was surprised when Jacob asked to come with me. We stayed silent as I drove, I wasn't even sure where I was headed, and we ended up at a local riverside park.

Putting the car in park, I switched off the engine. "I'm not sure how I feel about all of this," I said as the November wind off the river pushed against the car.

"Me either," Jacob sighed and let his head fall to the head rest. "This type of creepy stuff isn't exactly my strong point."

My nerves were stretched thin, and his words annoyed the hell out of me. "Yes, I'm sure this 'creepy stuff' is *very* upsetting to you," I said, sarcastically. Grabbing the door handle, I got out and slammed the car door shut.

Jacob exited from his side of the car. "What was that comment supposed to mean?" He walked around to the front, standing next to me.

Losing my temper wouldn't help, I knew. "I *meant* that I'm sure the discovery of a wise woman's prophecy—one that involves both yourself and your son—would go way beyond your comfort zone."

"Honestly, it weirds me out to know that someone from a hundred and seventy years ago foresaw us, and knew our fate. But I'm not *upset*...not really."

Weirds him out. I cringed at his choice of words. Why I was so disappointed in his reaction, I couldn't say. Hadn't I known all along what his true feelings were? I blew out a long, frustrated sigh.

"What?" he asked.

I lifted my face to the cold wind coming off the river. "Jacob, I'm sorry if you're frightened by all of this."

"I didn't say that," he shot back.

"Fine." I rolled my eyes. "Uneasy, concerned...whatever. I know these particular sorts of subjects make you uncomfortable."

"Subjects?" He folded his arms. "I'm not following you, Cammy."

I tossed up my hands in frustration. "For the past few weeks I've been very careful to avoid any conversation with you that involves the paranormal, occult, or magick."

"You have?" He blinked. "Why?"

"Because you've made it abundantly clear that you're very *uncomfortable* with it."

"I thought—"

"That what?" I cut him off. "That my magick was some fad, or hobby I'd lose interest in?"

"No." He frowned.

"What am I even doing here with you?" I said. "Why am I wasting my time with a man who doesn't believe in magick? I was a fool to try and build a relationship with someone who refuses to accept the most elemental part of *who I am!*"

"I knew you were holding back," Jacob said. "All this time I thought you were being cautious and taking things slow because I'm a single father."

"A single fath—" I cut myself off and narrowed my eyes at him. "How dare you say that! Jaime is an amazing little boy. You on the other hand—you're an idiot!"

"I guess you told me." Jacob struggled against a laugh. When I glared, the lone light in the parking lot sizzled out, and he quickly wiped the smile off his face.

"Damn it." I tried to yank my temper back in line.

"I had no idea that you felt like you couldn't be yourself around me. I'm sorry." He clasped my shoulder gently. "No wonder you're angry."

Silently, I struggled against tears of frustration.

"I thought you'd talk to me more about magick when *you* were ready," he said, threading his fingers through my hair. "I admit that I *have* been nervous, Cammy. But not for the reasons you thought...I was afraid that I'd say something wrong, or ask a stupid question and offend you."

"You were?"

He tipped my face up. "I was," he said and kissed me gently.

"For goddess sake." I said after his kiss. "We're both idiots." With a sigh I leaned my forehead against his chest.

"I suppose we should have sat down and had an honest conversation," he said, running his hand over my back, "...instead of talking around the subject."

"Probably." A weight I'd been carrying lifted. "I have to confess though, I don't like the idea that someone or something has been setting us up, or pulling the strings, stacking the deck...*whatever* you want to call it."

Jacob tipped my chin up so our eyes met. "What do we do now?"

"Well, I'll tell you this much," I said, trying to sound matter-of-fact. "I'm not going to be beholden to some old prophecy, and neither do I expect you to be. I have goals for my future and business timeline in place...No one but me decides my fate, not even some ancestor from a hundred and seventy years ago."

"I never believed in fate before," Jacob said quietly. "At least not until I met you."

I tipped my head to one side. "What exactly are you saying, Jacob?"

"I may not understand magick, or this prophecy we're a part of, but maybe it's not up to us," he said. "What if this was all written in the stars?"

"Then watch me re-write them," I said. "I chart my own course and make my own choices, thank you very much."

"I thought that way too, once," he said. "But the truth is, Cammy, you're here in my heart."

"What, now suddenly you're a romantic?" I asked.

"I always have been," he said and leaned in for another kiss. "I guess I did too good of a job covering that up."

"Let's not get carried away," I said, holding him off with a hand to his chest. "Jacob, we need to be rational."

Jacob smiled. "What if you're my destiny?"

He pressed a kiss to my forehead. "What then?"

"Talk of destiny from the skeptic?" I narrowed my eyes. "Are you feeling well?"

His slow smile should have clued me in, but I was too wound up and nervous to put it together. For the first time in my life my intuition let me down. Because I never would have predicted what he was about to do. Jacob grabbed ahold of my jacket, hauled me to my toes and proceeded to kiss the hell out of me.

His hands were everywhere and after a heartbeat, I returned the favor. We strained against each other even as the cold wind whipped around us.

"Cammy," his voice rumbled in my ear. "What do you say? Let's get carried away."

"Damn it," I half laughed-half groaned in frustration. "There's no privacy here."

Jacob tipped his head meaningfully toward the car.

"No," I shook my head. "I'm not having sex with you in the back of my car."

He pressed his hips against mine making my breath catch. "Are you sure?"

"Stop that," I said, breathlessly. "I can't think

when you do that."

He chuckled. "Then I must be doing something right."

"Where could we go to be alone?" I asked him.

"I have an idea," Jacob said, and made a suggestion that had me smiling.

"Are you sure we'd have privacy?" I asked as the wind whipped around us.

"I am," he said. "Trust me."

In a few minutes I pulled in the back entrance of the garden center. Quietly we exited my car and Jacob took my hand in his, leading me to the large greenhouse that was situated to one side of the parking lot. He unlocked the door and we slipped inside. While he re-locked it, I waited, and my eyes began to adjust to the lack of light. Being so dark, the scent of earth, growing plants and flowers surrounded me.

"This is wonderful," I told him.

"I thought you'd like it." He kissed me again. After a moment he lifted his head. "Come with me," he said, leading the way between the rows of the plants. I followed him as Jacob made his way to a work station. Before I had the chance to look around too much, Jacob's mouth was on mine. I felt him shrug off his coat and heard it drop to the ground. Our clothes were gone in moments, and the air was warm, fragrant and soft.

His hands were everywhere and his mouth trailed after. We paused only long enough to grab the condoms I had in my purse. When he tugged me down to the ground with him, I lay back willingly on his coat, but was surprised to feel a cushioned surface beneath us. I patted around wondering what it was.

"It's a work matt," Jacob whispered, kneeling between my legs.

"Aren't you clever?" I managed to say as he dealt with the condom. Then he caught my hips in his hands. "Jacob," I groaned as he pressed forward.

"Hang on," he warned me as I wrapped my arms and legs around him. "Because, Cammy, I do my very best work around plants."

***

We spent all night in the greenhouse. It was

crazy, fun, and romantic. Eventually we let each other sleep, and I woke up, tucked against his side, to the sound of Jacob's alarm on his phone. I opened my eyes and a pale pre-dawn light was coming through the curved plastic walls of the greenhouse. I turned my head and discovered that we were surrounded by poinsettias. There were hundreds of them, all arranged on tables in rows of red, white and pink.

I sat straight up. "Gorgeous."

"Yes, you are." Jacob's voice was husky.

I climbed to my feet with a slight groan. Sleeping on a rubber work matt was hardly ideal...then again we hadn't slept very much. "Look at all the poinsettias," I gasped. "I had no idea..." Fascinated, I walked over to the first table and ran my fingertips over the edges of the bracts of a hot pink poinsettia. "Did you know the *Euphorbia*, is indigenous to Mexico, and was sacred to the Aztecs?"

Jacob walked up behind me and dropped a kiss in the spot between my neck and shoulder. "No I didn't." He began to nibble on my neck. "Tell me more."

I leaned back against him. "The poinsettia is used as the birth flower for the month of December, and in the language of flowers it symbolizes happiness, success and celebrations."

"They must be working, because I'm feeling pretty happy." His hands wandered over me. "You look like a faerie walking around naked and surrounded by flowers."

"Well now that I can actually get a gander at you," I said, stepping deliberately back, "you're pretty spectacular yourself." In fact, I damn near purred at seeing his lean muscles, broad shoulders and a lightly furred chest. I let my eyes wander lower over his narrow hips, and saw for myself that he was indeed 'happy' to see me.

"Cammy," his voice was a low rumble.

"Yes?" I reached up with both hands to scrub at my hair, watching as his eyes followed the lifting of my breasts. "Did you want something?" I asked innocently, leaning against the wooden table with the flowers at my back.

"You," he said and reached for me.

A while later, I managed to stagger over to

my clothes and get dressed. I knew the man was strong, but he more than proved it by taking me while he stood upright in the middle of the rows of the greenhouse. I grinned over at Jacob while he buttoned his shirt. "I'm never going to look at poinsettias the same way again," I said.

"There's that," he said. "But I bet I'm going to get a hard-on every time I walk in this greenhouse from now on."

I snorted out a laugh. "Max is going to wonder about you."

We managed to leave the garden center well before anyone arrived to work for the day. I dropped him back at his family's house at dawn, and he hesitated before getting out of the car.

"Is there someone we can ask about the prophecy?" Jacob rested his hand on my thigh. "Someone with a different perspective?"

"I don't know." I blew out a long breath. "I'll talk to Gran this morning, and maybe I could ask Gabriella. She reads the tarot. Perhaps she can help us figure this out."

"What, and you *don't* read tarot cards?" Jacob sounded shocked.

I did a double take at the easy way he talked about the prophecy and tarot cards. "No," I said slowly. "I'm no good with the tarot deck."

Jacob grinned. "You're blowing your image, Camilla." He reached over and gave me a kiss. "I'll miss you." He climbed out of the car, bent over and spoke before he shut the door. "I'll call you after work. But if anything pops up, shoot me a text and keep me in the loop. Okay?"

"I can do that," I said.

He smiled and shut the door, and I pulled away from the curb. The drive to the farmhouse was a short one, and I was feeling wonderful. I strolled up the back steps, enjoying the buzz of a long night with an energetic and talented lover, and let myself into the kitchen of the farmhouse.

I moved noiselessly up the back stairs and went straight for the shower. The hot water helped the muscles in my back and legs. I started to chuckle as I thought about how they'd come to be stiff and sore. Still, I couldn't seem to wipe the satisfied grin off my face when I went down to the kitchen after getting dressed for the day.

I was thinking about nothing more than a large cup of tea when I snapped on the overhead kitchen lights and discovered Gran sitting at the kitchen table as if she was waiting for me. "Jeez, Gran!" I pressed a hand to my heart.

CHAPTER TEN

"Camilla Jane." She gave me a regal nod.

"Why are you sitting here in the dark?"

"I've been watching the sun rise, and waiting to speak to you."

I raised an eyebrow at her. "I hope you're not planning on giving me a lecture about staying out all night."

"Hardly." Gran's voice was as dry as toast. "Did you enjoy yourself?"

"Yes, I did."

"Good," she said. "Maybe now the two of you can move forward now, instead of staying in one place."

"We'll see," I said, and went straight for the kettle to start a pot of tea. "I'm glad you're awake, because I wanted to talk to you about that prophecy you mentioned."

"Yes?"

I selected a couple of mugs and brought them to the table. "Some things have come to light since yesterday, and I'd like your opinion on them."

"Of course." She inclined her head.

I filled her in on the journal entries Jenna Ames had shared with me and handed her my phone. "I took photos of Mary's journal yesterday."

Gran studied the pictures I'd taken. "Remind me what the ghost said to you when you were a teenager?"

"She said, *the prophecy awaits*."

"This may prove helpful," she said, and picked up an old book that had been resting in her lap.

"What's that?" I asked.

Gran handed me the slim volume. "It belonged to Victoria Midnight."

I noted that the cover was a faded, pale pink. I scanned the title. "An old book of love poems?"

"Victoria Midnight used that as sort of a

journal or a diary," Gran said. "It was among her most cherished possessions. If you look, you will see her notes and thoughts written in the margins."

I flipped open the book and studied the pages. The notes were written randomly in all directions, and from my quick perusal I found that some entries were listed with dates, while others were not. "What's the overall time period for these entries?"

"They vary," Gran said. "Starting in 1845 and continuing through 1855. I think you should go through these today. They may hold some of the answers you are searching for."

Gran didn't have much else to say, and her uncharacteristic silence made me realize that I should do as she suggested, immediately. After breakfast, I took the book to my room and began to study it. It didn't take long before I was sitting at my desk, taking notes on my computer, and trying to reorganize the dated entries in a chronological order. The other entries I organized by theme.

Victoria *had* written down her prophecy to Mary Ames, and it matched word-for-word with the entry I'd photographed the day before. But other than that, nothing else seemed to line up, or connect. It was a mish-mash of information, visions, and ramblings.

After a few hours, I stopped and rubbed my eyes. The best I could say about the old book was it contained dozens of original poems by Victoria Midnight. Even after reading her entries and trying to shift them into some sort of order, her thoughts were vague and unclear. Some were blatantly magickal—and read more like spells—while others made no sense at all.

"I suppose it's too much to ask, that your prophecies would make sense." I blew hair out of my eyes and rubbed at the tension gathering in my neck and shoulders. There was one poem/ entry that stuck out more than the others. I fretted over it and carefully copied the entry down to save in my computer files.

There are four stars of magick that shine
from a Midnight sky,
While three have been together, one was
hidden from their sight.
Though the search was in vain, love will
always find a way,

*This fact will be made known to her on the
saddest of days.
From the farthest western lands, the star
must journey home,
To claim her place, no longer to wander...lost
and alone.*

I sighed over it, wondered if I was falling down the rabbit hole—so to speak, and finally admitted to myself that I wouldn't solve this puzzle in a single day. Setting the book aside, I decided to take a break and emailed copies of the photos from Mary Ames' journal to myself, and to Philippe.

I printed the photos out on Dru's printer and tried again after lunch from a different angle, hoping to match another of Victoria's ramblings to the entries recorded by Mary Ames, or perhaps to our own family tree.

I was interrupted from my research later in the day by Drusilla who'd taken a break from her writing and Gabriella who'd come over to discuss Thanksgiving dinner. Gabriella and Philippe were hosting, and she was taking care of the turkey, potatoes and the stuffing. Dru had offered to bake three pies, while Garrett and

Brooke were going to contribute by bringing cheese and crackers for snacks before dinner. That left me with making casseroles and the vegetables.

After the food assignments were divvied up, I brought my sisters up to speed on what I'd recently learned. While Gabriella made herself at home propped up on all the pillows on my bed, Dru sat at the foot. I rolled my computer chair over and spread all the paperwork out on the bed to show them the research I'd done thus far. I shared my frustration in trying to reason out what appeared to be the irrational ramblings of an ancestor.

"Listen to this," I said to Gabriella and Drusilla, "I think Victoria may not have been all there."

Drusilla frowned. "What do you mean?"

"This poem for example." I pointed out the one about the four stars, waiting while my sisters read it.

"Perhaps she was a romantic." Gabriella sighed as she went through the book. "She was single her whole life. Maybe she was simply unhappy and lonely."

"Do you think the poem was about herself?" I said, feeling a buzz of excitement. "You know what? I thought about this earlier, but now I bet it *is* about her." I pointed to the family tree. "Victoria had two sisters *and* a brother. That must be the four stars."

"Her brother was our great-great-great grandfather," Drusilla said eyeballing the family tree for herself. "The other siblings all were married... Everyone except for Victoria. I wonder why?"

"Maybe she never found a man who could accept her and her talents." I heard myself say it, knew it to be true, and instantly felt sympathy for Victoria.

"Maybe not..." Gabriella's voice was thoughtful.

"What do you mean?" I asked.

"The book of poems has a dedication inside the front cover. And the handwriting is *not* the same as Victoria's."

"Really?" Dru asked.

"It does?" I frowned. "I studied the book for hours and never noticed it."

"Look." Gabriella motioned for us to both

come closer. "A few pages were stuck to the cover and I peeled them off. See what's written underneath?"

I leaned over. "*To my darling Victoria,*" I read the inscription out loud. "*Forever yours, P M.*"

Gabriella shuddered. "I've got this feeling in my gut. I wonder..." Her eyes were large in her face as she looked from Drusilla to me. "I think that P M stands for Pierre Michel."

"Oh shit." I shivered in response to her words and took the book back. "That makes for a horrible sort of synchronicity."

"What if Pierre Michel fought his arranged marriage because he was in love with someone else?" Gabriella rested her hands on her baby belly. "Say for example, Victoria?"

Drusilla held out her hand for the book. "Pierre Michel was forced to marry Bridgette, wasn't he?"

"That's how the story goes." Gabriella nodded. "His father had insisted on the match because the Ameses were wealthy and the dowry was sizeable."

I smirked. "While our family either worked

on the railroad, the river barges, or were farmers. It's a safe bet there would be no dowry —of any size—from a Midnight bride."

"Not to mention," Dru said, setting the book down with the papers, "if everyone in the village knew Victoria was a Seer that would have made her unacceptable to a family hoping to raise their status by marrying their sons off to wealthy, connected brides."

"What a horrible way to live." I sighed.

Drusilla shrugged. "For influential families in those days marriage was more about business contracts and advancement than love."

"As much as I like this theory," I said, "it's simply that. A theory. We don't have any proof."

Gabriella pulled her cell phone out of her purse. "Before I leave I'm going to snap a picture of that inscription," she said. "I'm not sure if Philippe has any samples of Pierre Michel's handwriting...but we could check."

"Yes and see if they match," I said, gathering up the papers and notes.

"Ella..." Drusilla leaned forward. "Are Max and Nicole coming for Thanksgiving?"

"They sure are," Gabriella said. "Philippe's grandfather arrives from France on Tuesday. He'll be joining us as well.

"Good," Dru said. "I'm looking forward to seeing Henri again. Cammy, are you going to bring Jacob to Thanksgiving?"

The papers I'd been stacking went flying. Drusilla had totally caught me off guard. "Er... I don't know." Embarrassed at my overreaction to her question, I busied myself tidying back up the notes.

"He and Jaime are more than welcome," Gabriella said smoothly.

I found that both of my sisters were grinning at me. "Cut it out," I said. "Just because you're both engaged doesn't mean I'm jumping on the bandwagon any time soon."

"Of course not." Dru brushed her long hair back. "We all know you have that business strategy firmly in place. Upsetting the carefully laid plans to open your own shop simply would never do."

"Right," Gabriella said with a straight face. "Gotta stick to that all-important schedule."

Drusilla nodded in agreement. "Otherwise

the world could end."

"Organization brings me joy," I said, sticking my nose in the air.

"Virgo!" Dru coughed.

I scowled at them both as they burst out laughing. "I'll ask Jacob," I said. "He probably already has plans though."

Gabriella got up and pressed a kiss to my cheek. "The more the merrier."

***

It ended up that Jacob's parents were going out of town to visit his older sister and her family for the holiday. Since the garden center was typically crazy busy on Black Friday with holiday tree, poinsettia and greenery sales, Jacob wasn't going with them.

Which meant my lover and his son were coming to Thanksgiving dinner. And to be honest, I wasn't sure how I felt about that. It was such a 'we're a couple' thing to do. Then there was the whole ghost/ ancestors/ prophecy issues. *Come have Thanksgiving dinner with us in the haunted house where one of your relatives disappeared and/or died,* I thought.

That was a hell of an invite. Who wouldn't be nervous about it? To be fair, Jacob had handled himself very well the last time he was in the house...and yes, we'd recently cleared the air between the two of us. But I worried nonetheless.

Desperate to keep from constantly fretting over it all, I threw myself into full soap making mode. Gift baskets were the hot item right now and I wanted to be ready for the holiday shopping season. Jacob had a busy week as well. I didn't get the chance to see him for the next few days, but we spoke on the phone and texted each other often.

The night before Thanksgiving, I double checked every single ingredient I planned to use in my vegetables and casseroles only to discover that the fried onions I'd planned to use for a topping had a warning that they had been manufactured on the same equipment as other products containing nuts.

That terrified me, so I tossed the unopened package out immediately and replaced them with a bread crumb topping. It shook me so much that once I had everything prepped I rushed to the phone, my heart pounding, and called Max, Garrett and Gabriella to remind them that Jaime had a nut allergy.

Max had been delegated to bring dinner rolls, but he promised me he would double check the ingredients on the package. Gabriella told me she wasn't using nuts in anything, but that she'd make certain there were no sorts of nutty snacks or any type of chips fried in peanut oil. Garrett said he would triple check all the cheeses and crackers they were bringing. Garrett assured me that there would be no accidental cross contamination with the party tray as he would re-wash it by hand immediately.

Feeling better, I trooped down to the kitchen to talk to Dru. To my surprise Drusilla took my warning as a personal affront to her culinary skills.

"Relax," Drusilla said, rolling out her pie crust. "I was planning to do pumpkin, apple and cherry pies."

"You won't be able to use almond extract in the cherry pie filling as you normally would." I warned her. "I can run to the market and get more frozen cherries if you need me to."

"Camilla." Dru stopped and glared at me. "I won't need them. It's fine. I don't have to use almond extract in the cherry pie. Lemon juice and nutmeg will work beautifully as well. Trust me, I am aware of how severe nut allergies can be."

"Well I..." I wrung my hands, caught myself and straightened my shoulders. "Okay. I only wanted you to be extra careful."

"And I will be." Drusilla pointed her doughy finger to the back door. "Now get out of my kitchen. Go see Jacob or something, because all of this anxious hovering is getting old."

"I'm not anxious," I argued. "Besides it's a family kitchen." Muttering, I grabbed my jacket and went out the back door. I drove over to Jacob's house, intending to ask him more about Jaime's allergies... It never hurt to be prepared.

I knocked on the front door and Jacob answered. "Hi." He smiled. "I didn't expect to see you tonight."

"I wanted to double check that Jaime doesn't have any other food allergies," I said, sounding a tad desperate.

"Come in." Jacob pulled me inside. "Jaime went to bed about a half hour ago."

The house seemed different without his parents at home. A football game was on, but the sound was down very low. "I called my family," I said, "and warned all of them about his nut allergies."

"Thank you." Jacob led me into the family room. "Gabriella knew, but I appreciate you being so thoughtful."

"Do you have an Epipen?" I blurted out.

"Of course." He smiled. "I keep one in my truck and I carry one with me when we go out. Don't worry."

I felt slightly ridiculous standing there while he smiled at me. "I had a scare earlier, when I saw that the topping I was planning to use on a casserole might contain nuts. Nevertheless, I tossed it and used something else."

"Yeah, that was smart." Jacob nodded. "We have to read *every* label and check all ingredient lists around here."

I suddenly realized I probably seemed slightly manic to him. Embarrassed, I cleared my throat. "I'm sorry Jacob, I shouldn't have shown up unannounced. Not to mention grilling you about your own child's allergies." I began easing toward the door. "I'll let you get back to your evening. Sorry to have interrupted. I was —"

"Worried," Jacob said, catching my hand.

I blew out a long breath. "Yes. That, and I was nervous about tomorrow anyway."

"About what?"

"You and me, Jaime, the family, the prophecy..." I stopped and closed my eyes. "It sort of all caught up with me and I panicked."

Jacob pulled me into his arms and kissed the top of my head. "You gave yourself a nice little anxiety attack didn't you?"

"I suppose I did." I lifted my face and he pressed a kiss to my mouth.

"I think you need a distraction," Jacob said and began unbuttoning my shirt.

"Hey," I said. "I'm all for distractions. But we can't with Jaime upstairs, can we?" God I wanted to but I told myself to be practical.

"You bet we can." Jacob kissed me again. "Besides, I want to make love with you on something soft."

I eyeballed the big sectional sofa across the room. "That couch does appear to be pretty comfortable," I said, unsnapping his jeans. "But I have to ask. Do you have any plants around here?"

"Hmm?" he asked, confused.

"Well, you've already proven you do good work around plants." I tugged his zipper down and grinned. "I wanted to make sure you had the environment you needed."

With laughter, we undressed each other and fell to the sofa.

***

I wondered how many years it had been since the mansion on the hill had hosted a big family dinner within its walls. Gran and I had been up at the mansion since noon giving Gabriella and Philippe a hand. Drusilla, Brooke and Garrett arrived at two, Max and Nicole arrived shortly thereafter, and Jacob and Jaime were due to arrive at any minute.

Pacing the decorated lobby on the first floor,

I kept watch out the window. I pulled down the long sleeves of my navy shirt and brushed off the front of my jeans. I'd dressed for comfort today since I knew I'd be hauling dishes, setting up the table in the dining room, and helping with whatever task I was assigned.

With a mixture of relief and nerves I finally saw Jacob's truck roll up the drive. I lifted my eyes to the ceiling. "If you're listening Bridgette, I'll take it as a personal favor if you would behave yourself today."

There was no 'answer' from the ghost but I honestly didn't expect one. I took a deep breath, opened the door and stood waiting for them. Jaime's feet had barely hit the ground before he was running full throttle to me.

"Happy Turkey Day!" he yelled, throwing his arms around my legs for a hug. "Is Claude here?"

"Who?" I gave the child a hug.

Jacob followed his son at a more leisurely pace. "Claude is his imaginary friend," he stage-whispered.

"Oh," I said. "I see." I kept an easy smile on my face even as I recalled that Philippe's ancestor was named Claude. Deliberately, I changed the subject. "What's this?" I pointed to the bouquet of fall flowers Jacob held. "Are those for me?" I asked.

"No, sorry." He bent down and kissed me hello. "They're for Gabriella."

"Oh," I said. "A hostess gift. That's nice of you."

Jacob pulled me in closer. "I was thinking about getting you some pink poinsettias."

"Are you trying to turn me on?" I whispered back.

"Dad!" Jamie's voice came impatiently from the stairway. "Miss Ella has pumpkins *inside* her house!"

"Are you ready for all of this?" I asked Jacob.

"Your family doesn't worry me Camilla." He hooked his arm in mine and we started up the staircase together.

The formal dining room table had been rescued from somewhere in the old house, and it practically took up the entire space in the kitchen and adjoining living room. It had taken two of Gran's old lace tablecloths to cover it.

Drusilla had created a pretty display down the center of the table with white mini-pumpkins, ivory candles and autumn foliage. I lit the candles for her, admiring the blue willow china my sister had reclaimed. Ella had even whipped up some cloth napkins on her sewing machine in a deep blue linen as a final touch to the table.

While the setting may have been formal, the atmosphere in the room and the people gathered around the table were anything but. Garrett poured all the adults a glass of wine and Philippe made a toast to friends and family. The food was enthusiastically passed around and conversation flowed.

Philippe held court at the head of the long table with Gabriella at the foot. I sat to Philippe's left with Jaime between Jacob and me. Max sat next to Jacob, and Nicole was at the end of our side of the table seated on Gabriella's right.

On the opposite side of the table, Brooke sat between Gabriella and Garrett with Drusilla on her fiancé's left. Gran sat next to Dru and Henri finished out the twelve of us by sitting between Gran and Philippe.

"You've got a full table, Philippe." I gave him an elbow nudge. "But you're going to need more leaves in it pretty soon."

He smiled. "There are more. Besides, there will be thirteen of us next year."

"I bet you there will be fourteen," Gabriella spoke up, causing the table to fall to silence.

"What do you mean, *ma belle*?" Philippe grinned at her. "I was with you for the last ultrasound. We are having only one."

Gabriella smirked at Max and Nicole. "I noticed Nicole was looking a little peaked, *and* she's not drinking her wine."

Nicole pressed her hand to her lips trying to cover a smile.

Max leaned forward. "How did you know, Ella?"

Gabriella tilted her head. "It takes one to know one. So, how far along are you?"

"Eight weeks," Nicole said. "We were going to keep it to ourselves until the first of the year."

"Aww." I was unable to stop my grin. "Honeymoon baby?"

"Apparently so." Max chuckled and shook

his head. "I should have known better thinking you all wouldn't...Well, *know*." Max grinned at Gabriella.

"Congratulations," Philippe raised his glass to the couple.

Wine and water glasses were raised in a toast, and when Jaime asked for more turkey dinner resumed.

After dinner the cleanup began. Gabriella ordered the men out and not one of them complained as they went to the third-floor tower to watch the football games. Gabriella and Brooke put away any leftovers, Dru loaded up the dishwasher with pots, pans and utensils, and I volunteered to start washing by hand whatever was left over—mainly the antique Blue Willow.

It didn't take long, and I chatted easily with Nicole and Gran as they dried the plates. Once we were finished Gabriella went to take Nicole upstairs to show her the nursery. Brooke Gran, and Dru headed off to join the guys. I dried my hands and flipped off the kitchen lights, intending on joining everyone in the tower. But when I hit the staircase to go up I heard a child's laugh.

At first I thought it was Jaime, but the child was younger and his coloring was all wrong— and so were the clothes. The pants came to right below his knees. *Breeches,* I realized.

My mouth dropped as the ghostly boy smiled at me and then he rushed down the stairs toward the lobby.

CHAPTER ELEVEN

Chills broke out on my arms as I hustled down the steps after the apparition. By the time I hit the first floor the lights had begun to flicker. I watched him zip off to the western wing of the house and I snagged my black jacket from the coat rack in the lobby and followed him, shrugging the coat on as I moved.

The boy's laughter floated behind him while his image drifted down the main hall and then went right up the western staircase. I paused at the base of the stairs, knowing there was no electricity running in the upper floors of this section of the house.

"*Attrape-moi si tu peux!*" His voice floated down to me.

"Catch me if you can," he'd said, and the French phrase didn't strike me as charming. Instead it made my blood run cold.

I picked up a candelabra that my sister had worked into another display on a side table and reached for the lighter in my pocket. I lit the tapers and decided to track the ghost. The thought of my sister following a ghost-child through her house or even Jaime coming into contact with it pushed me into action. Quickly I went up, and as I gained the third floor—there he stood. Very corporeal and at the top of the staircase.

"*Qui es-tu?*" I asked who he was in French and wondered if that would help him reply, but instead of answering he took off again faster than humanly possible and disappeared down the hall.

My pink chucks were noiseless as I followed him. I went to the end of the hall, stopping when I heard voices, and had to psych myself up to see who or *what* was speaking. A door stood open and I walked to the entrance. What I saw had me almost dropping the candleholder.

I hadn't entered an old dark room, for the

past had super-imposed itself on the present. The room was bright and two young boys were running around playing with a ball. A woman with blonde hair sat in a rocker, nursing an infant. She smiled serenely even as the other boys ran roughshod across their beds and all around the nursery.

*I'm witnessing the past...*I realized. *It's postcognition—a psychic vision of an event from the past. I'm seeing a memory that the house held on to.*

The scene suddenly changed. Now the boys were sleeping in their bed, and the baby lay in his crib. A woman with long, dark hair walked in and stopped to check on the children. It was Bridgette Ames. I recognized her from the daguerreotype. Bridgette smiled down at the oldest boy and ran a hand over his curls. She tucked in the second boy, checked over her shoulder, and an expression of fear crossed her face. Quickly she rushed from the room.

"Holy crap." I staggered and grabbed ahold of the doorframe as a third scene appeared. A man with dark hair walked to the far side of the room and all the furniture was covered in dust sheets. He knelt down, his back to me, and I couldn't make out what he was doing. He stood slowly and straightened his vest.

With a start, I grasped that he was dressed in all black—mourning clothes maybe. There was such sadness stamped across his face that I reached out to him, even though I know I couldn't help. I was seeing the past, and whatever I was seeing was over and done.

I blinked and found myself back in the present, standing in the middle of an old, dark, unheated room whose walls were covered in the remnants of silk wallpaper.

"I don't understand," I said to whatever force had allowed me to witness those moments in time. "Why have you shown me this?"

I jumped hard when a small yellow ball rolled across the floor. It moved past my feet and came to rest in the far corner of the room. Exactly in the same spot where I'd "seen" the man kneel.

I went over to the ball, to kneel myself, and discovered several little cars and a play fire engine. They were modern, and I knew they must belong to Jaime. He'd said something about giving his toys to the lady so she wouldn't be lonely.

Gently, I set the candelabra down on the floor. I reached out and ran my hands over the wall, but nothing felt loose. I checked the baseboard and the rosette at the edge of the closet trim shifted. I dug my fingernails in, pulled, and to my surprise the trim fell off revealing a small niche.

Gingerly I reached in and my fingers bumped into something solid. I pulled out a heavy metal tin. It was roughly five or six inches square and it was covered in grime.

I caught movement out of the corner of my eye and whipped my head around. Bridgette Ames stood to my right. Her hands were folded at her waist, she had a calm smile on her face, and was waiting and watching.

I fell back, landing on my butt. "Is this your dowry?" I asked her.

She didn't answer but my instincts said that it was, and I immediately tried to open the tin. I broke a few fingernails in my attempts but the tin was rusted shut.

"Cammy?" Jacob's voice came from the hall.

"Are you up here?"

"Jacob!" I called back. "I'm in the last room on the right. Hurry!"

I could hear footsteps as he ran, yet I kept my eyes on the apparition, wondering if she would fade when her descendant arrived.

"Jesus!" Jacob skidded to a stop in the doorway. "You're not alone."

"Nope."

Bridgette drifted closer and Jacob hurried to my side. "Are you hurt?" he dropped beside me. "It's freezing up here."

"No, I'm not hurt." I reached for him automatically. "How did you know I was here?"

"It's the weirdest thing, but Jaime told me his imaginary friend, Claude, said you needed my help. Jaime said that I'd find you in the room with all the little boys."

"He was right," I said. "This room used to be the nursery, and Jacob, *I've found something.*"

"Those are Jaime's toys," he said spotting the collection. "How did they get all the way up here?"

"That's not what I found." I handed him the heavy tin.

His eyes grew large. "Do you think that's..."

"Only one way to find out," I said. "Can you open this?"

He glanced at the apparition once, then reached into his pocket. "I carry a multi-tool. Let me try."

"Bridgette, do you know who this man is?" I asked, as Jacob worked on the tin.

"Why are you talking to it?" Jacob whispered. "Do you think she might actually answer?"

"You never know," I said. "And you should say hello, she's *your* Aunt."

Jacob peeked up at the apparition again. "Hello, Aunt Bridgette. I'm..." he stopped and cleared his throat nervously. "I'm Jacob Ames. My great-great-great grandfather was Jonah."

Bridgette nodded her head. *Jonah...* The ghost whispered.

Jacob cringed at the sound. "That's right," he said anyway.

I gave his shoulder a bolstering pat. "You're doing great."

Jacob bent his head to concentrate on opening the tin. He managed to cut through the old metal and then pull off the lid.

Inside was a flat wooden case with an ornate letter 'A' carved in the top. I caught my breath as I saw it. "By the goddess," I whispered.

"We should open this together," Jacob said, setting the metal top of the tin aside.

"I'd be honored to." I smiled at him and we carefully lifted the wooden lid of the case.

There, on a bed of old crumbly velvet, was Bridgette Ames' dowry. The amethyst parure that had been lost for one hundred and seventy years was now found.

"It's real," Jacob said, touching the largest stone in the bracelet.

"It certainly is." I smiled at him.

Jacob stood and helped me to my feet. He surprised me by taking a step toward the ghost. "Maybe you can rest now that we found it."

The apparition shook her head, and Jacob looked back at me. "Is there something you can do, Cammy? Something to help her go on her way? She shouldn't be stuck here wandering like this."

"I can try," I said to him. "If you're sure?"

"I'm sure." Jacob nodded. "Do whatever you

can."

Stepping forward, I raised up my own personal energy and held out my hands. "Bridgette Ames," I said firmly. "Your spirit is free. Be at peace and roam no more." The flames on the candelabra flared bright as I continued. "I accept that my part in the prophecy is fulfilled. Two sons of the Ames clan and a daughter of Midnight have worked together. Jaime showed you kindness, and Jacob believes in more than what he can always see."

Jacob took one of my hands. "Keep going," he urged, and stood by my side.

The candles snapped and crackled, the flames growing taller as we stood together. I pushed on, determined to live up to my destiny. "With love I send you to the afterlife, Bridgette. Go and be at peace in the arms of your loved ones."

Bridgette smiled at the two of us, and with a gentle sigh she faded away.

"Wow," Jacob whispered as the candle flames dropped back to normal. "I just saw that happen, you helped her cross over. I *felt* your magick."

"Are you okay?" I asked him.

"You're amazing," he said, and gave me an enthusiastic kiss.

As we kissed, the bottom of the metal tin clattered to the floor. I bent over to retrieve it. "Jacob, I said, looking inside the tin, "there's a letter."

Jacob retrieved the candlestick and I held the letter up to its light. "The name written on the front..." Jacob frowned, "Does that say Claude?"

"It does," I said. "I think this is the signature of Claude Marquette. It's dated November 14, 1847. That's exactly two weeks after Pierre Michel died."

Jacob blew out a long breath. "We should take this to your family."

***

Hand in hand, we walked into the tower room. Everyone fell silent as Jacob took the jewelry case to Philippe and Gabriella. "Cammy found this," he began.

"I had some help," I said, as Philippe opened the wooden case.

"*Mon dieu*," Henri breathed. "The jewels of Bridgette Ames."

"Did Claude and the lady show you where to find the purple rocks?" Jaime wanted to know.

"The purple rocks..." Gabriella's mouth dropped.

I held out a hand to Jaime. "How did you know about the purple rocks, Jamie?"

He raced over to me and I picked him up. "My friend Claude and the lady told me," he said.

"Out of the mouths of babes," Drusilla murmured.

"Claude talks funny," Jaime said. "He talks like Philippe's grandpa."

"French accent," Philippe realized.

"There's a letter as well," I said. "It's dated two weeks after Pierre Michel's death, and was signed by his brother, Claude. We found it under the jewelry case and within the tin."

"The letter can wait," Philippe said. "First, you tell me how this all happened."

Jacob and I sat on the sofa and everyone took

their seats as we explained what had occurred. The jewelry case was passed around and after Gabriella examined it, she set it gently down on the coffee table.

"I'd like to know what's in the letter," I said.

Jacob slipped an arm around me. "Maybe it will tell us what really happened to Bridgette."

Philippe opened it with care and handed the pages to his grandfather, Henri. "It's written in old French. My grandfather can translate this easier than I."

Henri Marquette slipped his reading glasses out of his jacket pocket and began to read aloud.

Claude Marquette, November 14, 1847

I have always considered myself to be a good man, but what happened in my home, what my family experienced has tested my morals and my faith in the divine.

It all began when my father brokered a marriage for my younger brother Pierre Michel. The bride was a young woman from an established family. My brother was not happy about being pressed into the marriage, however, he eventually was brought into line by the unyielding pressure of our father.

The bride was wealthy. Her family had made their fortune in the stone quarry and the railroad and her dowry was generous. Considering Pierre Michel's temperament, I am sure my father thought he was making the right decision, choosing a quiet, biddable girl from a prominent local family. Surely that would settle my brother down, putting an end to his carousing wild ways.

The first time I met Bridgette Ames, I had an uneasy feeling. She scarcely spoke above a whisper and rarely met anyone's eye when spoken to. The night the engagement was announced she stood in our parlor and held my brother's arm. Pierre Michel was a sought after young man, most young women in town would have been thrilled to have been engaged to him. Bridgette however, stood surrounded by people at her own engagement party and was silent, pale and shaking.

It was my own dear wife, Amelia, who pointed out to me the bride-to-be was barely touching Pierre's arm, while the groom was steadily getting drunk. When Jonah Ames, brother of the bride, toasted to the happiness of the couple Bridgette flinched and the mantle clock clunked a discordant sound and stopped working.

Almost as if it knew tragedy would soon follow.

The marriage was a disaster from the start. Although the new bride and groom were given rooms in the western wing, opposite where my family resided, they never seemed to be there, certainly they were never together.

For the few weeks she lived with us, my new sister-in-law preferred to come to the nursery and visit with the boys. She was there most days playing with them or reading to Claude Jr., or Henri. Bridgette would even hold the baby, Tomas, for Amelia, while she tended our other two boys.

One night my wife and I awoke to terrible screaming and shouting. We rushed to the opposite wing and when we found Pierre's bedroom door locked, I kicked it in. Bridgette was cowering in the corner of their bedroom while my brother bellowed curses at his wife, throwing whatever was at hand.

Pierre had another bad run of luck with the cards, and was searching for money, or anything that he could sell. He'd demanded that Bridgette give him her jewelry, and she had refused. I tried to restrain my brother, to calm him down while Amelia hurried to Bridgette. But when my brother turned his rage on the women I stopped him. I had never hit my brother before, and both of us were shocked. Pierre left the mansion, and Amelia tended to Bridgette.

The next morning, Bridgette brought me a small wooden box. She opened it, revealing her amethyst parure, and asked me to keep it safe for her, lest Pierre find it and sell it to pay his gambling debts.

I took the jewelry for safekeeping and offered to help Bridgette get away from Pierre. I would give her money to start a new life if she wished. But before we could put any plan into action, my sister-in-law vanished. We searched for her. Every day for months. But there was nothing.

My brother didn't seem to care. He was a stranger to us. He wandered around the house, drunk for the most part. As the weeks became months, the rumors grew ugly. Pierre was questioned about his wife's disappearance, and talk began in the village that he'd thrown her from the cliffs. Finally at the end of October he broke down.

When I pressed him for answers to what had happened to Bridgette all he would say is that it had been an accident. He never meant to hurt her. She had fallen, he claimed. Horrified, I demanded to know what he had done, but he lurched away and left the house. At dawn the following morning the constable arrived to inform me that my brother had died. He had overturned his carriage on the steep road of Notch Cliff. The newspapers called it justice, and the gossip in town was vile.

Now, it is a fortnight later. Amelia and I have made arrangements and are taking our boys away to France to escape the horrible rumors and lies about our family. I wanted to return the jewelry to the Ames family, but how could I?

I would have to confess how I came to have them, and what Pierre Michel had done and what little he had told me. There would be no comforting answers for Jonah or Mary Ames. I couldn't bring their sister back, and with Pierre Michel gone, I decided to hide the jewelry for safe keeping.

Perhaps one day, when the time is right, the truth will be known, and hopefully the jewelry will be given back to the descendants of the Ames family. I have done my best, and wish I could do more. But now I must put the needs and happiness of my own wife and children first. We depart at first light and I am glad to be leaving this place.

Henri cleared his throat and gently refolded the pages. "I am sorry, Jacob," he said. "There seems to be no clear answer as to what exactly happened to your ancestor."

Philippe picked up the wooden case and handed it to Jacob. "This belongs to you and your family."

Jacob accepted the case. "Thank you," he said.

It was silent for a long moment. Finally I had to break the tension. "Do we know how to throw a party, or what?" Everyone burst out laughing.

"That's a hell of a door prize," Gabriella said,

straight faced.

Garrett slipped an arm around Dru's shoulder's. "Dru and I will host Christmas at my house. No ghosts."

Drusilla smiled. "Good idea. Oh! I had planned to tell everyone after dinner, but we all got distracted. Garrett and I have set the date for our wedding."

"I'm going to be the maid of honor!" Brooke said excitedly.

"Please don't say the date you picked out is before June," Gran said.

Dru pressed a hand to her chest. "I'd *never* upstage my sister's wedding like that."

Garrett smiled at Gran. "We were thinking more along the lines of September."

"Three months apart then." Gran held up her empty wine glass. "I'd like a drink, please."

Henri moved to oblige her. "Do you need an escort to the weddings, Priscilla?"

Gran sent the silver-haired Frenchman a considering look. "Is that an offer?"

"I think our grandparents are flirting, *ma belle*," Philippe said to Gabriella.

Gabriella sipped at her apple cider. "I need a

drink," she muttered. "Or dessert."

Nicole perked up. "That does sound good. I've been craving sweets, terribly."

"Don't worry," Drusilla said to Nicole. "I made three different kinds of pie."

Brooke popped up. "I can serve the pie. I can do it."

"Knock yourself out honey," Gabriella said. "Everything is on the counter in the kitchen."

"Pie?" Jaime rolled off my lap and made a run for the door. "I like pie! I wanna help." He went barreling after Brooke.

I stood and held out a hand to Jacob. "Why don't we go see if the kids need any help?"

He rose. "I'm on my way."

"Listen you two, please don't get into any more adventures before dessert," Gabriella said with a smile.

I tossed her a wink over my shoulder. "I'm pretty sure that we're done with any adventures and prophecies for a good long while."

***

The Ames family had the amethyst parure

cleaned, repaired and appraised. The amount of money the jewelry was worth was stunning, and they insured it accordingly. When word got out that the jewelry had been found, the newspapers had run a story on both the Marquette and Ames families.

There had been quite a few photos of Gabriella and Philippe, along with Jacob and his family. Afterward, Gabriella had come up with the idea to make a public room in the mansion that would be dedicated to local history of the village, the winery and the mansion, but would also focus on the history and contributions of both the Marquette and Ames families as well.

I finalized the paperwork for renting the building for my shop and signed the contracts in December. That gave me three weeks to have the shop ready to go before the "Eagle Days" in Grafton. The annual event kicked off each year in mid-January, and folks would come from all over the United States to see the bald eagles in their winter home. It was the perfect time to launch a business, as Ames Crossing was inundated each year by tourists.

The winery was gearing up as well, and Nicole had worked her PR magick and had a few wine tastings for private groups scheduled in the newly completed ballroom in the public side of the mansion.

Jacob had more free hours in the winter months, and I discovered for myself that the man was good with his hands...as in woodworking and handyman skills. He rolled up his sleeves and helped me paint, build displays, and he and his father both pitched in, adding more lighting to the shop in areas where I needed it.

On weekends and evenings when Jaime wasn't in school he was with Jacob and me. The three of us had been inseparable since Thanksgiving, and things were going well. I hadn't calculated on falling in love with two 'men' at the same time, but as time went along, I came to realize that planned for or not...that is exactly what had happened.

Locking the door behind me, I stood bundled against the cold in a heavy black coat and pink scarf and studied my store window. It was all decked out for the winter holidays, and a banner across the top of the windows let folks know the shop was "Coming Soon".

I took a critical survey of my presentation. I'd draped white velvet over boxes and stands, making a multi-tiered display. On that, silvery pails of pastel pink and white bath bombs appeared to spill over and across the fabric. Stacks of my beautiful hand-made soaps and glass bottles of lotions and shampoos were displayed to advantage and framed my big *'Camilla's Lotions & Potions'* sign.

I'd wrapped some white LED twinkle lights among it all for sparkle, and to finish it off there were pots of pink and white poinsettias tucked around them. Their cheerful message of happiness, success and celebrations, was a subtle bit of wise woman's magick.

A pair of familiar arms wrapped around me. "Hello gorgeous." Jacob's voice tickled my ear.

I leaned back to give him a kiss. "Hello handsome."

"The display is amazing," Jacob said. "I'm damn proud of you."

"Thank you," I said. "And thanks for the poinsettias."

"I'm partial to the pink poinsettias myself."
Jacob rested his chin on top of my head. "I've
yet to figure out why that is."

I couldn't help but laugh. "They are
absolutely charming, *and* they add the perfect
festive finishing touch."

"Something about this time of year makes
you believe that anything is possible," Jacob
said as we walked hand in hand to his truck. He
stopped, pulled something out of his pocket,
and held it over our heads. "Well, would you
look at that?" He sounded surprised. "I wonder
where that mistletoe came from?"

"Jacob, you old romantic." I gave his fingers
a squeeze. "Did you know that the mistletoe is
called the Golden Bough? It was sacred to the
Druids, and in the language of flowers it means
—"

"I love you," he interrupted, and grinned
down at me.

My breath caught. "I love you too."

"So what does mistletoe mean in the
language of flowers?" he said. "Don't leave me
hanging."

"That the one who holds it can overcome

anything, and if you kiss under it...you'll forever be in love."

"Perfect," he said, and then he reeled me in with one arm and kissed me senseless.

EPILOGUE

Six months later...

The day of Gabriella and Philippe's wedding had finally arrived. I stood between Drusilla and Brooke in my blush colored bridesmaid dress on the restored western terrace of the Marquette mansion, watching as the couple exchanged rings. His, a simple brushed gold band, and hers was a thin golden eternity band sparkling with diamonds and sky-blue topaz.

Gabriella was beautiful in her new off-the-shoulder metallic lace gown. The floor length gown left her arms bare, featured a sweetheart bodice, and had an A-line skirt. The shimmery light blue color was perfect on her. Philippe was handsome as well in his tux of pearl gray with a white shirt and coordinating pale blue tie.

I glanced back at the wedding guests and smiled. Baby Danielle was sitting in Gran's lap. The baby's dark hair was accented with a stretchy headband that featured a pink ribbon rose. Danielle's dress was white and had a sweet explosion of a tiny tulle skirt. Nicole sat beside Gran, and her baby bump strained against the pretty spring green maternity dress she wore. She was jiggling a set of plastic toy keys to help keep my three-month-old niece entertained.

Beside them Jacob sat with Jaime—the two gorgeous males that I'd fallen head over heels with. Jenna and Jeremiah Ames sat behind them, and his mother was wearing the beautiful Ames amethyst collet necklace. She smiled and gave me a small wave.

Jaime, I noticed, was tugging on his bow tie, clearly unhappy with wearing it, and Jacob was mouth wateringly handsome in his navy suit. As I watched, Jacob bent over and whispered something into his son's ear that made the child grin, then he tossed me a wink.

I shifted my attention back to the bride and groom. The couple sealed their vows with a kiss and everyone let out a cheer. Drusilla handed Gabriella her bridal bouquet. My sister had chosen well for her bridal flowers. They were stunning with apricot roses, pale pink peonies, rose colored astilbe, silvery dusty miller, and soft white English roses. In the language of flowers the bride carried: charm, beauty, sophisticated pleasures, happiness and unity.

The couple began the recessional, pausing only long enough for Philippe to scoop up his infant daughter in one arm. Together, the family of three continued down the aisle.

Drusilla and Garrett followed. I partnered up with Max, and Brooke was escorted by Philippe's grandfather, Henri—who'd been delighted to stand up for Philippe as a groomsman.

Later, I was finally able to dance with Jacob in the ballroom. With a happy sigh, I leaned my head against his shoulder.

"This turned out to be a really nice place to hold a wedding," Jacob said. "Especially since the ghosts seem to be behaving themselves these days."

"I told you the haunting is over." I gave his fingers a squeeze. "Bridgette is finally at rest and the prophecy has been fulfilled."

"It still blows my mind that I played a part in all of this." He smiled down into my eyes. "That we both did."

Jaime came running over. "Hey! Dance with me too." He beamed up at us.

"Of course." I hitched Jaime onto my hip and pressed a loud kiss to his cheek. "Love you," I said to the little boy, making him giggle. The three of us danced together and it was wonderful, swaying to the music with both of my guys.

"You know," Jacob said a few moments later, "there's something Jaime and I have been wanting to ask you."

"Oh?" Jaime wanted to get down, and I set him back on his feet.

Jacob cleared his throat and Jaime smiled up at his father. "Go on, Dad," the boy said impatiently.

I realized with a start that the music had

stopped and the dance floor was suddenly clear of everyone except the three of us. I saw that Gran, Drusilla, Garrett and Brooke were standing at the side of the dance floor, watching. As a matter of fact, every single guest was smiling and viewing us rather expectantly. I shot a quick glance at the bride and groom. Gabriella was beaming and holding Danielle, and Philippe gave Jacob a 'go-ahead' nod.

"What are you doing?" I asked suspiciously as Jaime began to bounce up and down.

Jacob reached in the pocket of his suit trousers and pulled out a ring box. "Camilla Jane Midnight," he began.

"Oh my goddess." I pressed my hands to my mouth.

Jacob went down on one knee with his son standing beside him. "I love you. Will you marry me?" He opened the box, and I gasped.

The main stone of the ring flashed. It was a medium pink and fashioned in an emerald cut. Tiny diamonds sparkled along the platinum band. It was striking, gorgeous and unique. I shifted my gaze from the ring to the face of the man who knelt before me. "Is that..." I stammered a bit. "Is that a tourmaline?"

"It's a pink sapphire," Jacob said. "Obviously, I went for a pink stone."

"Say yes!" Jaime shouted, excitedly. "After you do, Miss Ella says we can have the cake!"

Overcome, I nodded my head. Everyone began to chuckle, and I started to cry happy tears. "Yes, yes, of course!" I managed to say.

A huge grin split Jacob's face as he stood. He took the ring out and slid it on my finger. "Love you," he said. "Let's be a family."

"I'd love to." I rushed into his arms for a kiss.

The wedding guests let out a cheer, and Jaime wrapped his arms around my legs, giving me a hug too. Jacob scooped his son up and the three of us embraced again.

We were promptly swarmed by the family. I accepted hugs and kisses from Jacob's parents, and from my own relatives. When I got to Gabriella, she confided that she and Philippe had not only known about the proposal—that she had helped Jacob choose the ring. It was *her* idea that Jacob should propose to me at the reception.

"Sneaky," I said, accepting her congratulatory hug.

I felt a tug on my skirt a few moments later. "Can we have the cake now?" Jaime wanted to know.

"You bet," I said, running my hand over Jaime's hair. "As soon as Gabriella and Philippe cut it."

Jaime clapped his hands. "They're going over to cut it now! I wanna watch." He dashed across the ballroom and went to stand with Brooke.

Eventually Jacob and I managed to steal a few private moments away from the other guests at the reception.

"I love you," I told Jacob as we stood together under the starry skies on the western terrace. Reaching up on my toes, I intended to give him a kiss. But before I could, a bright shooting star blazed across the sky and headed to the west.

"Look at that!" Jacob breathed.

I kissed him before the shooting star faded. "It's almost enough to make you believe in magick, isn't it?"

Jacob lifted my left hand, pressing a kiss to my fingers above the pink sapphire. "I don't need shooting stars to remind me that there's magick, Cammy."

"You don't?" I asked, admiring my engagement ring.

"No," he said, pulling me close. "All I need to see, is *you*."

The prophecy that had brought us together had worked its magick. Now, in the old house on the cliffs, where there once was pain and heartbreak—there was strength, family, hope for a bright future, and the most powerful force of all. Love.

The End

ABOUT THE AUTHOR

Ellen Dugan is the award-winning author of over twenty-eight books. Ellen's popular non-fiction titles have been translated into over twelve foreign languages. She branched out successfully into paranormal fiction with her popular *Legacy Of Magick, The Gypsy Chronicles,* and *Daughters Of Midnight* series. Ellen has been featured in USA TODAY'S HEA column. She lives an enchanted life in Missouri tending to her extensive perennial gardens and writing. Please visit her website and blog:

www.ellendugan.com
www.ellendugan.blogspot.com

Made in the USA
Lexington, KY
24 June 2019